CONTENTS

Christmas
WITH A
BEAR SHIFTER

KELSEY KARSON

Published by Dobson Ink
Printed in the United States of America
ISBN-13: 978-1-946474-40-7

CHAPTER 1
SILENT PINES

At the end of a long winding driveway, surrounded by towering pines heavy with snow, sat a small, rustic cabin. It was isolated and precisely what Maddie Garrett needed. When a friend of a friend presented the opportunity to rent the cabin for a few weeks, she didn't waste a moment, just threw clothes into a suitcase, grabbed her laptop, and left with her last shred of dignity. A six-hour drive north into the mountains seemed like the perfect way to spend the holidays. No more pitying looks, no more passing the office building that had been her life for the last six years, and best yet, she didn't have to return to the apartment she'd shared with Derek.

Merry Christmas to me.

Visible through the trees about a hundred yards up the hill was a large house, more of a lodge than a private home. Lucia had mentioned something about the main house, but explained that the property owner was hardly ever around. It didn't matter to Maddie as long as she got out of the city. She wasn't there to make friends. She needed to figure out what she was supposed to do with her life now.

Maddie climbed onto the porch, carrying the few groceries she

1

had purchased from the last big town and her suitcase. She grabbed the key under the mat and quickly unlocked the door before toeing off her soaked, snow-covered sneakers. The chill of the cabin hit her as her phone vibrated in her pocket. She set the groceries on the counter and pulled out her cell phone. Derek's name flashed on the screen.

> You can't just disappear like this, Maddie.
>
> We need to talk.
>
> Maddie, come on. This is ridiculous.
>
> I know you're upset, but ignoring me won't fix anything.

Message after message flooded her phone. "Why couldn't there be no service?" she muttered. She silenced the phone and tossed it onto the table. The whole point of this trip was to ignore her problems, not have them texting every five minutes.

The kitchen opened into the cozy living room, where a sectional sofa dominated the space in front of the fireplace, and the large glass windows offered a magnificent view of the Christmas tree farm that bordered the property. Yet what she noticed was the quietness. The silence was startling. No traffic or sirens that seemed to echo through the city round the clock. No neighbors arguing through the thin walls.

"This is what I need."

She glanced around the kitchen. The kitchen was updated and modern, though the cabin was rustic. Spotting the kettle on the gas range, she filled it up with water. Unpacking and exploring the rest of the cabin could wait until she had tea. With the kettle on the stove, she turned to the market bags and quickly put them away. The market was surprisingly well stocked, and she was able to pick up everything she needed. Allowing her to relax and enjoy her time away from civilization.

Pulling out the bakery box of fresh gingerbread cookies, she noticed the top one was cracked. Right in the middle of his chest, it was broken in two. "Just like me," she mumbled as she reached into the box. "How had I not seen this coming? At Christmas..."

The kettle whistled, startling her, and the gingerbread man fell to the counter, crumbling further. "Great." She pulled the kettle off and poured the water into the waiting mug before dropping a tea bag in.

"The cookie is just like my life, shattered." With her tea steeping, she gathered up the cookie crumbs and dropped them into the trash can.

A heavy knock rattled the cabin door.

Maddie jumped. She wasn't expecting anyone. She didn't even know anyone within a hundred miles, at least. A knock came again, hard this time, and impatient.

Brushing off her hands, she crossed over to the door. Rising onto her toes, she peered through the small window. A man stood on the porch. Tall, broad-shouldered, with dark hair that was dusted with snow. Dressed in a heavy work coat and boots, he had an expression that caught her attention. She could only describe it as thunderous and certainly unwelcoming.

She cracked open the door. "Can I help you?"

"What are you doing here?" His voice was rough, deep, and unfriendly.

"Excuse me?" She raised an eyebrow at him.

"What are you doing in this cabin?"

"I..." she bristled. "I rented it. Not that it's your business."

"From whom?" His jaw tightened.

"Lucia." She met his gaze. "I don't know what your problem is, but—"

"Lucia. Of course she did." He shook his head as he pulled his phone out of the pocket of his coat, jabbed at the screen, and pressed it to his ear.

She could hear the ringing, and ringing, but no answer.

The man stood there on her porch and lowered the phone from his ear, scowling. His gaze fixed on her. His eyes burned an unusual amber, almost gold, as tension carved sharp lines along his jaw.

"I'm Nico Matthews. I own this property. The main house on the hill, this cabin, and all the land you can see. My sister had no right... no right to rent this place out."

"I paid..." Maddie's stomach sank. "I paid her for the month upfront in cash."

"Figured." He dragged his hand through his hair, snow falling from the dark strands. "This is unbelievable. She knew..." Trailing off, he looked at her. "Look, Miss...?"

"Maddie Garrett."

"Miss Garrett, I don't know what my sister told you, but you can't stay here."

"Excuse me?" After a long, exhausting day of driving, her patience was thin. "I have a rental agreement, and I've already paid for a month stay. I'm not going anywhere."

"It's not safe."

She glanced around the porch, looking for anything that would make the place unsafe, because she had found nothing concerning inside yet. "Cabin looks fine to me."

"That's not what I meant." He stopped, brows furrowed. "There are things happening on this property. Especially in the winter. Potential dangers. I can't have a stranger—"

"Then your sister should have considered that. Take it up with her." She stepped back and started to close the door. "I'll be out of your hair in a few weeks. Until then, I'm staying."

He held up a hand, stopping the door before she could close it. "Miss Garrett—"

"Goodnight, Mr. Matthews."

For a long moment, they stared at each other. His eyes seemed to glow in the darkness, and her chest had a strange flutter, though she wasn't sure if it was from fear or something else.

"Lock your doors and don't go wandering around the property

after dark," he warned, stepping back. "If you see or hear anything unusual, you come straight to the main house. Understood?"

"What do you mean by unusual?"

Without answering, he turned and walked away, his broad form disappearing into the snowy darkness. With her heart pounding against her ribcage, she closed the door and locked it.

"What have I gotten myself into?"

She stepped away from the door and grabbed her phone from the counter with the intent to call Lucia and demand an explanation. Before she could dial, she noticed three new messages from Derek.

> Your mom is worried about you.
>
> Tell me where you are!
>
> Maddie, please.

"Forget it." She powered off the phone and put it down on the table again.

Instead, she grabbed her tea and headed to the living room to start a fire. Tomorrow she'd call Lucia. For tonight, she was going to pretend the angry, golden-eyed man and cryptic warnings didn't exist. She was going to enjoy her mug of tea, a fire, and try to remember what peace felt like. Even if it only lasted until morning.

CHAPTER 2
THE WEIGHT OF SNOW

S unlight streamed through unfamiliar windows. As Maddie lay there on the bed, surrounded by plush pillows and a thick comforter, the first thing she noticed was the profound silence and the deep snow blanketing everything in whiteness. After a disorienting moment, it all came rushing back to her. Renting Lucia's cabin, the drive, the angry man with golden eyes who'd appeared on her doorstep like some mountain hermit with a grudge.

She glanced out the window, out onto the rows of snow-covered fir trees. The morning sun glistens on the snow, making it glimmer like diamonds. Even the deep, untouched snow seemed magical. "I could get used to waking up to this."

She pushes back the covers and gets out of bed. It was the first day of her new adventure, and she would not waste it moping around in bed. She quickly dressed in the first thing in her suitcase, jeans and a red V-neck sweater.

Today, she had plans to explore the cozy town she'd glimpsed as she made her way to the cabin. What little she saw seemed to explode with Christmas cheer, maybe even enough to rub off on her. But first, she needed coffee.

As she made her way out of the bedroom, the chill of the cabin made her glance at the fireplace. The fire had died overnight, and frost decorated the inside of the windows in delicate patterns. She grabbed the quilt from the corner of the sofa and wrapped it around her as she made her way to the fireplace. Building a fire was one of the few skills her father had taught her during their childhood camping trips.

The first flicker of the flames licked the log, and she scooted closer to the warmth. Her phone, still sitting on the table, pinged. As much as she wanted to ignore it, she rose from the hearth, tugged the blanket closer to her, and stepped up next to the table. Grabbing the phone, she slid her finger across the screen. Not to find an emergency, but dozens of text messages. Two from her mother:

> Honey, Derek's called, looking for you. I know you need time, but call him.
>
> He's a good man who made a mistake. Give him another chance.

Maddie let out a deep breath as she squeezed the phone tighter. The rest of the unread messages were from Derek. Without reading them, she hit the delete button.

"Coffee," she mumbled to herself, setting the phone back on the table.

Walking around the kitchen bar counter, she took in the space. The cabin was small, but the kitchen seemed to be its heart. It was recently updated and even had a fancy coffee maker. She didn't need fancy, but she did need coffee. Caffeine was a necessity if she was going to respond to her mother and figure out her life.

She grabbed the ground coffee from the tin, measured it, then poured it into the filter and filled the water reservoir. All while her mother's message ran through her thoughts. *He's a good man who made a mistake.*

A mistake? A mistake was forgetting to take out the trash. It wasn't wasting six years in a relationship that he had no intention of taking further. She'd told him about her goals and what she wanted for her life. All the while, she believed they were on the same page. Yet, that clearly wasn't the case.

Her gaze fell on her cell phone before she shook her head. Her mother had always had a soft spot for Derek, but this time she was wrong. He wasn't a bad person, but there was no second chance to be had here. Not this time.

With enough coffee brewed for a cup, she hit the pause button and poured some into a mug before sliding the pot back under the drip to finish. Breathing in the bitterness with a hit of caramel, she made her way to the window seat, taking in the snow-covered landscape. The rows of pine trees, with a light dusting of snow on their branches, sparkled in the morning sun.

"I could get used to this view."

The main house up the hill was more visible in daylight. A sprawling log structure with a wide porch and smoke curling from the chimney. Movement caught her attention, and she glanced toward it to find Nico outside, splitting wood.

As she took a sip of the hot coffee, she watched him. From a distance, she could see the effortless power in each swing of the axe. Despite the cold, he'd taken off his coat, working in just a thermal shirt and jeans. The way he moved was fluid and precise, as if every motion were calibrated. He wasn't only strong, he was graceful. Certainly, something worth observing.

"Too bad he hates me." She tried to brush the thought off. He was just a guy. One angry, property-protective guy who clearly had issues with his sister.

The thought of Lucia made her set her coffee mug aside and grab her phone off the table. She scrolled through her contacts until she found Lucia's number and pressed call. It rang six times before going to voicemail.

"You've reached Lucia. I'm probably off having an adventure. Leave a message, I'll call you back."

"Lucia, it's Maddie. Your brother showed up last night and was...

well, he was surprised to find me here. He seemed pretty upset that you rented this cabin to me. Can you call me back to clarify what's going on? Thanks."

Hitting the end button, Maddie couldn't help but feel a little uneasy. Maybe the whole call was a stupid idea. What was Lucia going to say? *Sorry, I forgot to mention my brother's a controlling jerk who doesn't want anyone on the property.* If that was the case, why was Lucia even renting out the cabin?

Returning to the window, she found Nico stacking the wood with the same efficient grace. He paused, turning his head toward the cabin as if he sensed her watching. She stepped back quickly, heart hammering.

Get it together, Maddie. You're not doing anything wrong.

Dropping down onto the window seat, she tugged her laptop out of the bag she'd sat near the sofa the night before. Waiting for the computer to power up, her gaze drifted back toward the main house. Nico was no longer in sight.

Good, he'd have only distracted me anyway.

Connected to the internet, she pulled up a website and began her job hunt. Every posting was filled with the same dull corporate-speak: dynamic team, fast-paced environment, and self-starters. Everything she had before. Rather than fulfilled, it had left her hollow. She wanted a change.

"This isn't helping."

Needing to get out of the cabin, she set her laptop aside and stood. There was a little town not far. An outing could get her mind off what a disaster her life had become. She slipped on her boots and grabbed her coat.

The main street of Timber Ridge looked quaint and tourist-friendly. There also had to be a grocery store where she could pick up a few supplies to be prepared for the upcoming storm. More than that, it would allow her to explore and get out of her own thoughts for a bit.

As she buttoned her coat, she pulled open the front door, and the scent of pine and woodsmoke directed toward her. There was something welcoming about it. The driveway had recently been plowed. There was even a path to her car.

Did Nico do this? Why, when he wants me gone so much?

She was almost to her car when she heard the crunch of footsteps in the snow.

"Heading out?"

She turned to find Nico approaching from the direction of the main house. With the sun streaming down around him, he was even more striking. Dark hair that needed a trim, strong features, and those unsettling amber eyes. He certainly appeared to belong in these mountains, like he'd been carved from the same stone as the peaks surrounding them.

"I'm heading into town. I need supplies before the storm," she said, keeping her voice neutral.

"Timber Ridge?"

"Unless there's something closer?"

"No." He seemed to study her for a moment, something unreadable in his expression. "The roads are tricky with snow. Take it slow, especially on the curves."

Concern? From a man who tried to evict her. Interesting. She reached into her coat pocket, making sure her cell phone was there, just in case she ran into any issues.

"I'll be careful." She forced a smile onto her face as she pulled her keys from her coat pocket. "Thanks for the concern."

"Miss Garrett."

"Maddie," she corrected instinctively.

He started to turn around, but stopped. "Maddie."

The way he said her name twisted a knot in her stomach, and she glanced up at him.

"I'm sorry about last night. I was...well, you caught me off guard."

"I got that impression." With her gaze still on him, she reached out and grabbed hold of the door handle.

A hint of a smile touched his lips before it vanished. "My sister has a talent for causing chaos. But that doesn't mean I should have taken it out on you."

"Are you saying I can stay then?" Not that she was planning on letting him run her off, but it would certainly make things less tense.

"For now." His gaze focused on her, and the intensity from the night before was back. "But those warnings stand. Don't wander the property after dark. And if you see anything unusual—"

"I know, come to the main house. You mentioned that." She cut him off.

"I'm serious, Maddie."

"What exactly am I supposed to be looking for? Bears? Wolves?" She was half-joking, but the way he stared at her, his features blank, as if not wanting to give anything away, was unnerving.

"Something like that." He turned and started walking away before she could respond.

She stood there a moment, watching as his long strides carried him back up the hill toward the main house, before she turned and got into her car. As she started the engine, she forced herself to look away from his retreating back. *What did he mean? Were there really bears and wolves close enough to the house that she might encounter them?*

The drive to Timber Ridge was both beautiful and nerve-wracking. The mountain roads twisted and turned, with sheer rock on one side and steep drops on the other. The views, however, were breathtaking—endless forest, snow-capped peaks, and the bluest sky Maddie had ever seen.

Timber Ridge itself was picture-perfect. It looked like it came straight from a holiday movie, all decorated and perfect. The main street was lined with brick buildings adorned with evergreen garland

and twinkling white lights. In the town square stood a massive Christmas tree. Despite the cold and snow, people were out enjoying the town and shops.

She pulled into a parking spot near the town square, taking in the tree. The lights glowed among the snow-covered branches, and a song from some carolers drifted along the wind toward her. She wished she had time to wander through the stores of this quiet town, but with the storm coming and the roads already treacherous, she couldn't spend too much time.

Instead, as she walked past, she peered in their windows, making a mental list of the best-looking Christmas displays and baked goods. As she neared the general store, she spotted the hanging sign: Timber Ridge General, Established 1925.

As she stepped into the shop, the smell of cinnamon and coffee hit her. The store was larger than it looked from the outside, with aisles of groceries, a small café area, a few racks of clothes, and even a hardware section along the far wall.

"Everything a person could need," she mumbled to herself.

"Welcome," an older woman with steel-gray hair glanced up at her from behind the counter. "You're new in town."

"That obvious, huh?" She unbuttoned her coat.

"Small town." The woman smiled. "We notice new faces. I'm Kate Watson, and this is my store."

"Maddie Garrett. I'm renting the cabin on the Matthews' property for a couple of weeks."

Interest flickered in Kate's expression before she nodded. "Nico's place. How's he doing?"

"He's...fine, I guess. Haven't spoken to him much." She grabbed a basket from the door.

"I suppose not." Kate nodded. "He's a good man. Keeps to himself too much since Elena passed."

Elena. Maddie recalled Lucia mentioning Nico's late wife, but she'd been too focused on getting out of town to really think about it.

"He has a daughter, right?"

"Oakley. She's six and bright as a penny. If you ask me, that child needs more people in her life. Nico does his best, but..." Kate trailed off. "Listen to me, gossiping to a stranger. You need help finding anything?"

"No, thanks. I'm just stocking up on the basics. I'll wander."

As she shopped, she couldn't help but notice the other customers. They all seemed to know each other, greeting one another by name and asking about family members. Most gave her curious glances, as if they hadn't expected an outsider to be among them, but they were friendly enough.

Something felt different about the town, but she couldn't put her finger on it. Maybe it was just the isolation, the close-knit nature of a small mountain community. But the way people moved and the intensity in their gaze when they looked at her made the hair on the back of her neck prickle with awareness.

She gathered the groceries she needed and even grabbed a bottle of wine from the shelf before heading to the checkout. Unlike the city, there was no self-serve option, instead, Kate was there to ring up her purchases.

"This weekend starts our Christmas festival and market. You should come back into town for it. It's really something special. Lots of vendors, activities, and great food."

"I...ummm...I'll think about it." With a nod, Maddie gathered up her bags and headed for the door.

The Christmas market sounded nice. But with the looks she was getting from the residents, she wasn't sure she'd be as welcomed as Kate made it seem.

As she stepped out of the shop, her cell phone buzzed in her coat pocket. She juggled the groceries in one arm and pulled it out only to find Derek's name on the screen.

I miss you. Can we please talk?

She stared at the message for a long moment. Weeks ago, she

14

would have melted at those words. Now standing in a snowy parking lot in a town she'd never heard of until two days ago, Maddie felt nothing. Feeling guilty, she shot off a quick response.

I need more time. Please respect that.

How much time?

She stared down at his response for a moment before locking her phone and slipping it back into her pocket. "As much time as I want," she mumbled as she opened the back door and set the groceries down on the seat.

With snow already falling, she climbed into her car, started up the engine, and headed back to the cabin. She'd wanted to explore Timber Ridge, but between the storm and Derek, she'd lost interest.

"Maybe I will come back to town for the Christmas festival." Before heading out of town, she took one last glance at the massive tree decorated in the town square. "Now that I'm staying, I need a Christmas tree."

Even with the worsening roads, the drive back to the cabin felt shorter and more familiar. Maybe it was because she recognized landmarks, such as the twisted pine that reminded her of a dancer, or the outcropping of rock that resembled a bear's head.

By the time she pulled up to the cabin, she found a fresh stack of firewood on the porch, neatly arranged and covered with a tarp. Nico must have brought it while she was gone. For someone who wanted her gone, he sure tried to keep her warm and comfortable. With his cryptic warnings and kindness, she wasn't sure what to make of him.

With snow covering her windshield, she stepped out of the car, grabbed the groceries from the backseat, and headed inside. As she did, she glanced up at the main house. No sign of Nico, but smoke curled from the chimney.

The day had slipped by, and darkness was already settling over the land. Nico's words drifted through her thoughts. *Don't wander the property after dark.*

15

CHAPTER 3
OLD BLOOD

M addie didn't sleep well. Every creak of the cabin settling, every gust of wind through the pines, and every distant sound had her jerking away, heart pounding against her ribcage. She kept thinking about the noises she heard throughout the night, the heavy footfalls, that low rumbling her brain insisted was just wind, but her instincts screamed that it was something else. By the time dawn broke, she was exhausted and jittery from too much coffee.

She stood at the window, watching the sun paint the snow pink and gold, and tried to ease the paranoia she'd been feeling. She was a city girl unused to wilderness sounds, and Nico's warnings had unsettled her. It was probably nothing, just warnings about actual bears or mountain lions living in these mountains. Except there had been nothing normal about the way he looked at her when he'd given that warning.

Her phone vibrated across the coffee table, making her turn around and glance at the screen. Lucia. Setting down her coffee mug, she grabbed the phone and unlocked it. "Hello."

"Maddie! I just got your message. I'm so sorry about Nico."

"Your brother seemed pretty surprised to find me here." She dragged her finger along the edge of the table as she looked back out the window toward the main house.

Lucia sighed dramatically. "Nico is always surprised when I do anything. He thinks he gets to control every aspect of the property just because he lives there."

"He said he owns it."

"Technically, we both inherited it from our parents. The cabin is as much mine as it is his. He just conveniently forgets that when it suits him." There was an edge in Lucia's voice, one that hinted at old resentments. "Did he give you a hard time?"

"Said I couldn't stay." Maddie nodded as if Lucia could see it.

"Of course he did." Lucia let out a soft laugh. "You paid, so you have every right to be there. Nico's just...well, he's overprotective, controlling, and thinks everyone should live by his rules."

"He...um..." Maddie hesitated. "He mentioned something about it not being safe here."

"Oh, please. He's being dramatic. What, did he tell you there are wolves in the woods?" Lucia laughed, but it sounded forced, doing nothing to ease the tension in Maddie. "Seriously, Maddie, stay as long as you want. You said you needed this. You wanted a break from everything. Right?"

"Yeah, I do."

"Then don't let my brother bully you. And Maddie? I really am sorry. I should have given him a heads-up. I just...I didn't want to deal with him telling me no." Someone called Lucia's name in the background. "Look, I've got to go. But if he gives you any more problems, call me."

Before she could respond, Lucia hung up, leaving Maddie feeling marginally better. Whatever it was with Nico, it was just a family dispute, nothing sinister, and nothing she did. Nico was an overprotective older brother, probably used to making all the decisions. The strange sounds she heard during the night were just wildlife, nothing unusual. The odd atmosphere in town was just small-town closeness. Everything that seemed strange to her had a logical explanation if she only looked for it.

"If only I believed that."

She grabbed her laptop and tried to keep herself busy. This trip was supposed to clear her head and give her direction, but she also needed to find a job and a new apartment. So far, she'd tried to reach out to old contacts, but no solid leads. Leaving her to scour the internet in search of any position in her field to apply for. Slim pickings.

It was made more difficult by the fact that her thoughts kept wandering to the stack of firewood on the porch, to the amber eyes that seemed to glow in the darkness, to the fluid grace of a man splitting wood.

"This is crazy." She closed her laptop and stood. It wasn't snowing, and the wind had died down. The perfect time to explore the immediate area around the cabin. Nico had warned her not to wander around after dark, but he hadn't said anything about during the day.

She grabbed her coat and stepped out into the early afternoon sunlight. The snow was pristine, unmarked except for animal tracks. As she stepped off the porch, she followed a path that seemed to lead toward a creek she could hear rushing somewhere in the trees. The forest was beautiful, silent except for the occasional bird call and the whisper of wind through branches heavy with snow.

It didn't take her long before she found the creek, partially frozen along the edges as water flowed freely in the center. She stood on the bank, snapping photos with her phone, when she heard voices.

"I tell you, it was close. Too close to the houses."

"We'll set up patrols. We'll double them if we must."

She froze. Listening to the male voices coming from somewhere upstream. She couldn't see who was talking through the trees.

"What about the human?"

Human? Were they talking about her?

"I'm handling it."

Nico. She was certain that was Nico, she'd recognize that deep rumble anywhere.

"Really? From what I've heard, she's still at the cabin. That's a problem. You know the convergence is coming. If she's still here when—"

"She won't be."

"You sure about that?" a gruff voice entered into the conversation. "I saw the way you looked at her, and you know what that means."

"It doesn't mean anything," Nico said defensively.

"Brother, if she's your—"

"She's not," Nico snapped.

There was a long pause before the gruff voice spoke again. "Your bear thinks differently."

"My bear will deal with it."

Bear? Her pulse sped, but before she could think about what she heard, footsteps crunched in the snow, coming closer. She panicked and tried to back away quickly, slipped on the icy creek bank, and went down hard. Her phone flew from her hand to land in the snow.

"Shit," she hissed, scrambling to her feet.

"Who's there?" This time it wasn't Nico's voice. This one sounded younger, sharper.

She grabbed her phone and turned to run, but it was too late. Three men emerged from the trees. All tall, with broad shoulders. The youngest was maybe in his mid-twenties, with shaggy blond hair. The other was older and darker, with a scar across his left eyebrow. Then there was Nico.

"Miss Garrett." Nico stepped around the other two, his expression unreadable. "What are you doing out here?"

"Walking." She tried to sound confident despite her racing heart. "It's daylight. You said not to wander after *dark.*"

The blond man looked at Nico, his eyebrows raised. The scarred man crossed his arms, studying her with unsettling intensity.

"This is private property. The creek marks the boundary of the safe zone," Nico explained, ignoring the other two men.

"Safe zone?"

"The area around the cabin." He moved closer, his two companions flanking him. Intentional or not, the effect was intimidating. "Beyond this point, you could run into wildlife. Dangerous wildlife."

"Like what you were tracking?" The words came out before she could stop them. "The thing that was too close to the houses?"

All three men went still.

"You were listening," the scarred man said flatly.

"I didn't mean to. I was just taking pictures, and I heard voices—"

"How much did you hear?" Nico cut her off, his voice controlled, but there was something underneath it. Worry. Maybe fear.

"Not much. Something about patrols and...and a convergence?" She looked between them. "What's going on? Is there actually some kind of danger here?"

"This is exactly what we didn't need," the blond man muttered under his breath.

Nico shot him a quelling look, then turned back to Maddie. "There's been some unusual animal activity in the area. We're taking precautions. That's all you need to know."

"What about the part with me being a problem?" She focused her attention on him.

"You're not a problem." His jaw tightened, as if he didn't believe the words himself.

"That's not what it sounded like."

"With all due respect, Miss Garrett, you're out of your depths here." The scarred man spoke up. "There are things about this place, this community, that you don't understand. It would be better for everyone if you finished your vacation and went home."

Something in his tone made her spine stiffen, and she stood up straighter. "Are you threatening me?"

"Grayson." Nico's voice cracked through the stillness. "Back off."

"Just being practical." Grayson held up his hands.

"I'll handle it."

"Will you?" Grayson's gaze flicked between Nico and Maddie, and concern etched the lines around his eyes. "Because the longer she stays—"

"I said I'll handle it."

The two men exchanged a look, then the younger one shrugged. "Your call, boss." With that, he disappeared into the woods.

The one with the scar, she now knew, was Grayson, who shook his head and followed the younger man into the woods. They moved with surprising speed and silence.

Now alone with Nico, she glanced toward him. "Boss?"

"I manage the property. They work for me." He moved closer, and she had to tilt her head back to meet his gaze. "Maddie, I need you to trust me. Stay close to the cabin. Don't go wandering, day or night. Also, don't listen to conversations that aren't meant for you."

"Kind of hard not to when you're having them in the woods where anyone could overhear."

"We didn't expect you to be out here."

"It's the middle of the afternoon!"

"I know." He dragged his hand through his hair, a gesture of frustration she was starting to recognize. "Look, I'm not trying to scare you. But there are legitimate dangers in these mountains. Things that—" He stopped himself. "Just trust me. Please, Maddie."

She studied his face, trying to get a read on him. There was genuine concern, maybe even fear, in his eyes. But she wasn't sure if it was for her safety or something else.

"What did he mean about you looking at me?" The question slipped out before she could stop it.

"Nothing." Nico's expression tightened, as if hiding behind a blank slate. "Grayson reads too much into things."

"Nico—"

"I should walk you back." He started toward the cabin, clearly expecting her to follow.

She stood there for a moment, frustration warring with unease. Everything about the situation felt wrong. The cryptic warnings, the overheard conversation, the way all three men had reacted when they'd seen her. Something was going on, but she couldn't put her finger on it.

My bear will deal with it. What did that even mean?

But Nico was waiting, and the shadows were already getting longer. Night would be upon them before long, and she didn't want to be out there alone in the dark, not with the sounds from last night still fresh in her memory.

Reluctantly, she followed him back to the cabin in silence.

At the porch, he paused. "I know you think I'm being paranoid or controlling, but I'm asking you, please be careful. Stay inside after dark. Keep your doors locked."

"You're really freaking me out, you know that?"

"Good, maybe you'll listen."

He turned to go, but she reached out and caught his arm. The contact sent a jolt through her. His body heat was remarkable, radiating through his coat as if he were running a fever.

"Are you okay?" She pulled her hand back. "You're really warm."

"I'm fine." He stared down at where she'd touched him, and the rawness in his eyes made his breath catch.

The moment stretched between them, tension building like a thunderstorm gathering strength.

"Daddy!" A small voice hollered from up the hill.

Nico stepped back as the little girl came running down the path from the main house. Dark braids flying, her pink puffy coat flapping behind her, and boots with sparkles and unicorns on them.

"Oakley, wait—" Nico started, but she'd already reached them.

The girl stopped in front of Maddie, tilting her head up with a huge smile. "Hi! You're the lady staying in the cabin. I'm Oakley. I'm six. What's your name?"

"I'm Maddie. It's nice to meet you, Oakley." Despite everything, she found herself smiling down at the young girl.

"Oakley, you can't just run off like that," Nico said, exasperated.

"But Daddy, I wanted to meet her!" Oakley turned back to

Maddie. "Are you staying for Christmas? Do you like Christmas? We're going to have a gigantic tree and everything. Daddy promised."

"I..." Maddie glanced at Nico. "I might be here for Christmas."

"Great! Do you want to see my room? I have a rock collection, a dollhouse, and a picture of my mom—"

"Oakley, Miss Garrett, is busy." Nico's voice was gentle, yet firm.

"Actually, I'd love to see your room sometime." Maddie wasn't sure why she said that, but there was something about Oakley's bubbly personality that made her not want to disappoint the girl.

"Really?" Oakley's face lit up with a big smile.

"Yes."

"Can she come now, Daddy? Please." Oakley bounced on her feet, waiting for his answer.

He looked trapped between his daughter's hopeful expression and his own clear desire to keep Maddie at arm's length. "Not today, sweetheart. Miss Garrett just got back from a walk in the woods. I'm sure she wants to rest."

"Okay." Oakley's shoulders sank. "But soon?"

"Soon," she promised.

"Come on, Oakley, it's time to go back to the house." He placed his hand on her shoulder and led her back up the hill. Oakley turned and waved enthusiastically. Maddie waved back, watching them go.

She saw Nico's hand on Oakley's shoulder, protective and gentle. Saw the way he bent down to listen when she spoke to him. Most of all, she witnessed the love in every gesture. Whatever was going on there, whatever secrets this place held, Nico Matthews was a father who clearly adored his daughter. That much, at least, was real.

With one last glance toward the main house, she headed inside and locked the door as instructed. Through the window, she could see lights come on in the main house as dusk settled over the mountains.

My bear will deal with it.

She slipped off her jacket and turned toward the kitchen island where her laptop waited. She opened her laptop, pulled up a tab, and searched: Timber Ridge unusual animal activity.

Nothing useful came up.

When she tried wildlife in Timber Ridge, Colorado, the only results she received were generic, about elk and mountain lions.

On impulse, she tried one last time: Timber Ridge, Colorado legends.

The first result came from a blog by a folklore enthusiast. Most of it was standard stuff about the mining town and frontier history. But one paragraph caught her attention.

Local legends speak of the Winter Guardians, protectors who have watched over the mountains for generations. Locals are very hush-hush about it, but I got the impression it wasn't just folklore, at least not to them. An elderly resident told me, 'Some families carry the old blood. They keep us safe.' But when I asked what she meant, she would only say, 'You either know, or you don't. If you don't, it's better that way.' So, I'll leave it to you. Is there something more to Timber Ridge?"

"This is crazy." With her pulse racing, she closed her laptop. She was letting the isolation and the stress of the past few weeks make her paranoid. "There's no such thing as—"

A howl split the night. Long, mournful, and too close to the cabin for comfort.

She stood there frozen, listening, as another howl answered the first. Then another.

But beneath them, she heard something else, a roar that sounded almost like a bear.

"A bear?"

CHAPTER 4
OAKLEY'S VISIT

Morning light held silence, and no more mysterious howls or unexplained sounds. In the daylight, Maddie's nighttime paranoia seemed ridiculous. Had she let her imagination run wild? Too many true crime podcasts and suspense novels, mixed with not enough sleep.

With coffee in hand, she opened her laptop, determined to focus on something productive. Her savings would only last so long, and she needed a job. Anything. But so far, the city only seemed to offer her the same type of position she had left behind. While she needed work, she wasn't certain she wanted to go back to the mind-numbing corporate offices again. What she wanted was something new, something exciting, but what that was, she wasn't certain.

She scanned the job boards again when a knock at the door echoed through the space, making her jump. As she rose from the sofa, she closed her laptop and set it on the coffee table before glancing at the fire. "Wood," she mumbled to herself as a reminder she needed to restock the basket next to the fireplace. If she was going to the porch, she might as well make herself useful.

She opened the door and found Oakley. The reminder to grab wood was already slipping away.

The little girl was bundled in her pink coat, a knit hat with a pom-pom pulled down over her braids. She had a smile bright enough to light up the gray morning as she held out a plate covered with aluminum foil.

"I brought you cookies!" Oakley exclaimed.

"Oh." Maddie couldn't help but smile. "Thank you, Oakley. That's really sweet of you."

"Dad said I shouldn't bother you, but I wanted to say hi. We made cookies last night, but he wouldn't let me eat all of them, so there are many left over. I thought you might like some because you're all alone down here, and I know when I'm alone, I'm sad, especially before Christmas," she rambled on, barely pausing for breath.

"I definitely like cookies, so thank you. Would you like to come in?"

"Really?" Oakley's eyes widened.

"Really. It's cold out here."

Oakley practically bounced inside, looking around the cabin with curiosity, as if she hadn't been there in a while. "It's so cozy. When Aunt Lucia lived here, she had all this fancy stuff everywhere. You're so much neater."

"Your Aunt Lucia used to live here?" Maddie couldn't picture Lucia, the city girl she knew, living here in the middle of nowhere. Lucia seemed to enjoy the city life too much for this.

"Uh-huh. Before she moved to the city. Daddy says she wanted a different life." Oakley set the plate of cookies on the counter and pulled off her gloves. "Can I take off my coat?"

"Well, of course, how else are you going to enjoy your cookie?" Maddie pulled back the foil, revealing homemade chocolate chip cookies. Some were slightly misshapen but smelled amazing. "Did you help make these?"

"Yep! I did all the mixing. Daddy even let me crack the eggs and everything. One of them got a shell in it, but we fished it out." She hung her coat carefully on the back of a chair, then climbed up onto the couch. "What are you doing?"

"Job hunting, actually."

"What's that?" Oakley asked.

"Looking for a new job. I used to work for a company that planned events, like parties and conferences. But they had to let some people go, and I was one of them."

"That's sad." Oakley's face scrunched up in sympathy. "Did you like your job?"

Surprised, Maddie paused. "You know, I'm not sure. I was good at it, but now I don't think I liked it very much."

"Then it's good you don't have it anymore. Now you can find something you like. Plus, it brought you here."

"You're right." She let out a soft laugh at Oakley's simple attitude toward how life worked.

"I'm right a lot. Daddy says I'm too smart for my own good. So why did you come here? To Aunt Lucia's cabin?" She swung her legs, which didn't quite reach the floor.

"A lot of things changed in my life recently, and I needed to get away."

"Like what?"

"Well..." She grabbed the plate of cookies and brought them over to the sofa where Oakley sat, holding them out to her. "I lost my job, and my boyfriend and I broke up. Seemed like the perfect time to get away for a bit."

"Did you love him?" Oakley asked, taking one of the chocolate chip cookies.

The innocent question caught Maddie off guard for a moment. "I thought I did, but now I'm not so sure."

"Daddy loved my mama. Say he still does, even though she's in Heaven." There was no sadness in Oakley's voice, just stating the facts, but there was a shadow that passed across her face. "I don't really remember her. Just that she used to sing to me."

"I'm certain she was wonderful." She grabbed her own cookie before setting the plate on the coffee table.

"Daddy says she was the best person he ever knew and that I look like her." She took a bite of her cookie before touching her braid. "He does my hair every morning. It's crooked sometimes, but I don't complain. He tries hard."

Maddie smiled at the idea of Nico bending down to carefully braid his daughter's hair. "I bet he does a great job."

"He does okay, but he can't do French braids. Aunt Lucia tried to teach him, but his fingers are too big. At least that's what he said. Can you do a French braid?" Oakley looked up at her with hope in her eyes.

"I can."

"Really?" Oakley's eyes lit up. "Could you teach me? I want to learn so I can do it myself."

"Sure." She took a bite of the cookie and nodded.

"Could you do it now?" She was already scrambling off the sofa. "I have a brush in my coat pocket. Daddy always makes me carry it because my hair gets tangled when it's not braided."

Before she could respond, Oakley retrieved a small brush and was back on the sofa, vibrating with excitement.

"Okay, turn around." She dropped her cookie onto the foil and took the brush from Oakley.

She settled behind Oakley and gently removed her hat, then began carefully unbraiding her hair. It was thick and beautiful, with a slight wave. "Your hair is gorgeous."

"Daddy says it's like Mama's. I got my eyes and hair from her, but I got Daddy's..." She trailed off before quickly adding. "His nose. I got his nose."

"You know you're pretty brave coming down here by yourself." Maddie started the French braid, working slowly.

"I'm not allowed to go far from the house by myself. But the cabin is on the property, so it's okay. Besides, I can—" She stopped abruptly.

30

"Can what?"

"Umm...I can see the house from here. So, it's safe." Oakley shifted as if uncomfortable.

It seemed like an obvious cover, but Maddie let it go and focused on the braid. "So, you go to school?"

"Yeah, Timber Ridge Elementary. There are only sixty-three kids in the school. One of them is my best friend, Emma. Her grandma owns the general store in town. Have you been there?"

"I was there yesterday, and I think I met her grandma. She was very nice."

"Everyone in Timber Ridge is nice," Oakley declared. "It's a good place to live. Safe and friendly and..." Oakley twisted back to look at Maddie. "You should stay here forever. We need more people, especially nice ones, and you, Miss Garrett, are nice."

"I don't know about forever, but I'm here for a couple of weeks." She smiled.

"What if you like it here? Maybe you decide this is where you want to be. Will you stay then?"

"Oakley—"

"We don't get a lot of new people here in Timber Ridge. You're so nice, and Daddy likes you. I can just tell, even if he's being grumpy about it—"

"Oakley Marie Matthews!"

Both of them jumped, and when Maddie turned toward the voice, she spotted Nico standing in the open doorway, snowflakes melting in his dark hair. His expression was a complicated mix of concern, exasperation, and something that appeared to be panic.

"Daddy! Miss Maddie is doing my hair!" Oakley turned her head, messing up the half-finished braid.

"I can see that." Nico stepped further inside, his presence somehow making the cabin feel smaller. "I told you before, I don't want you bothering Miss Garrett."

"I'm not bothering her," Oakley defended. "I brought her cookies, and we're having girl time."

"Oakley—"

"It's fine," Maddie cut him off before he could continue. "She's been wonderful company."

Nico's jaw tightened. His gaze drifted from his daughter to her and the scene before him. Cozy domestic scene with Maddie braiding Oakley's hair, cookies on the table, and something in his expression cracked. Longing. But just as quickly as it appeared, it was gone. "Oakley, we talked about this. Miss Garrett is staying at Aunt Lucia's cabin for vacation. She doesn't want a six-year-old pestering her all day."

"I wasn't pestering! Tell him, Miss Maddie."

"Nico, she really wasn't." Maddie looked at him. "I was job hunting, and honestly, she's a much better use of my time."

"See?" Oakley beamed triumphantly. "I'm not being a nuisance."

Nico rubbed his temples as if he were fighting a headache. "Oakley, go put your coat on. I need to get back to the fence line, and you wanted to come along."

"But Daddy, my braid."

"Now, please." The firmness in his tone made it clear there was no room for argument.

Oakley's shoulders sank with disappointment, but she climbed off the sofa and retrieved her coat.

"Thank you for the cookies, Oakley."

"You're welcome." Oakley's voice was small and disappointed.

As she buttoned her coat, Nico stepped closer to Maddie, lowering his voice. "I'm sorry. She's been...curious about you. I should have kept a better eye on her."

"She's six. Kids are curious."

"She's also lonely," he admitted, and from the look in his eyes, it was clear it cost him something. "It's mostly just me and her up at the house. We have extended family around, but it's not the same as..."

"As having a mom?"

His gaze met hers, and the raw pain in his eyes made her chest ache. "Yeah."

"Nico, she's wonderful. You're doing an amazing job with her."

He swallowed hard. "Thank you."

Oakley finished putting on her coat and was standing near the door, shoulders slumped.

On impulse, Maddie stepped away from Nico and knelt down to Oakley. "You know what? Maybe you could come back another time, and I'll braid your hair. Then you can tell me more about school and your friend Emma. Deal?"

"Really?" She stared up at her, a smile tugging up the corner of her lips. "Daddy, did you hear that? Miss Maddie said I could come back!"

"We'll see," Nico said, but his voice had softened. He met Maddie's gaze, and something passed between them. Connection. Gratitude. That same pull she'd felt before, electric and undeniable. "Say thank you to Miss Maddie."

"Thank you, Miss Maddie." Oakley threw her arms around Maddie in an impulsive hug.

She hugged the young girl back, surprised by the fierceness of it, but also by how much Oakley's affection affected her.

"You smell nice, like wildflowers," Oakley said as she pulled back, grinning.

"Oakley." Nico shook his head, embarrassed.

"What, Daddy? She does!" She grabbed her father's hand. "Come on, Daddy. You said we had to check the fence line."

As they started to leave, Nico paused in the doorway. "The cookies...they're safe. In case you were wondering. No weird ingredients or anything."

"I wasn't worried." She laughed.

He paused as if he wanted to say something else, but Oakley tugged at his hand.

"Daddy, come on."

"I'm coming." He let Oakley pull him outside but glanced back at her once more before heading up the path to the main house.

With her heart beating faster than it should, she closed the door and moved toward the window to watch them walk back to the main house. Oakley chattering and gesturing animatedly, as Nico followed her, patient as the devoted father he clearly was. As they neared the top of the path, he picked her up and swung her onto his shoulders. Oakley's laughter carried across the snowy yard, drifting toward Maddie, as the first snowflakes began to fall again.

She touched the glass, watching them.

A single father doing his best to raise a daughter alone, who looked at her like she was a blessing and a curse all at once.

Daddy likes you. I can just tell, even if he's being grumpy about it.

She stepped away from the window and picked up the cookie she'd abandoned. It was delicious. Rich chocolate and perfectly chewy. Made with love by a father and daughter who were starting to work their way under her skin.

CHAPTER 5

BOUNDARIES AND CURIOSITY

Over the next few days, Maddie tried to establish something resembling a routine, anything to reclaim her life. Mornings began with coffee by the window as the sun painted the mountains in pinks and golds. The job hunt began afterwards, though she realized that every listing felt like taking a step backward, returning to a life that no longer fit.

Maybe her days in the city were over. The isolation in the cabin should have felt oppressive, but instead it felt like breathing room. Something she didn't experience in the city. Making her think that relocation, not specifically to Timber Ridge, but somewhere quiet, was just what she needed.

She hadn't seen Oakley since her cookie delivery, but she often spotted her playing in the yard of the main house. Each time, the little girl would wave enthusiastically. Maddie always waved back, smiling at the unbridled enthusiasm.

Nico was more reserved. He'd been around the property, chopping wood, checking fences, tending to the tree farm, basically doing whatever needed to be done. Sometimes he'd acknowledge her, while other times he seemed to deliberately avoid looking in her direction. The hot-and-cold routine was starting to drive her crazy.

Every day, her cell phone rang while she was making lunch, and Derek's name would flash on the screen. Usually, she'd hit the decline button right away, but today she stood there, watching the screen, as it rang a couple of times. She picked it up, and instead of declining the call, she answered it.

"Hello?"

"Maddie." His voice was filled with relief. "I was starting to think you were never going to talk to me."

She moved to the window, watching the snow fall. "Derek, I told you I needed time."

"I know. I just...Maddie, I hate how we left things. Can we talk? Like, really talk?"

She could picture him in his apartment, the one they used to share. He'd be wearing his navy sweater, the one that brought out his eyes. He'd have the earnest expression he got when he was trying to fix something. Even as she pictured it, it all felt very far away, and the emotions she had come there with seemed gone.

"What do you want to talk about, Derek?"

"Us." He let out a deep sigh. "What happened? I've been thinking a lot, and I realize I made a huge mistake. I got scared. Your job downsizing, the pressure...all of it. I wasn't handling it well. I took it out on our relationship."

"You broke up with me a week after I lost my job."

"I know, Maddie, and I'm sorry. It was terrible timing. But it wasn't really about you losing your job, it was about me freaking out about the future, stability, and all that adult stuff I've been avoiding."

Leaning back against the counter, Maddie closed her eyes. A month ago, this call would have made her heart race with hope, but now it just made her tired. "Derek—"

"Hear me out, Maddie. I miss you, I miss us. This apartment is lonely without you, and everything feels wrong. I get that I hurt you, but we had two good years together. That must count for something."

She realized there was no 'I'm sorry' or even a hint of remorse in his tone. "It counts, but—"

"Come home, Maddie. Let's talk face-to-face. We can work this out."

"I..." She glanced down at the kitchen countertop, as if it held the answer. "Derek, I don't know if there's anything to work out."

Silence descended on them, thick enough to cut stone.

"Do you...is there someone else?" Derek asked.

An image of Nico flashed through her mind. His amber eyes, the heat of his body when they touched, and the way he looked at her when she'd been braiding Oakley's hair.

"No." It was technically true, even if she felt a connection with Nico. There wasn't someone else, just perhaps a possibility of something.

"Then what is it?"

"I don't know," she admitted. "I need space to figure out what I actually want."

"Have you? Figured it out yet, Maddie?"

She looked out at the mountains, and the main house caught her attention again. "I'm getting there."

"Maddie, we were good together, and we could be again. Don't throw that away because you're scared or confused or—"

"I'm not scared," she said quietly. "For the first time in a long time, I'm not scared, and maybe that's the problem."

"What does that mean?" The annoyance was clear in Derek's tone.

"I was comfortable with you, but I don't think I was happy. Not really. I don't think either of us was. Our relationship just felt safe."

"That's not fair." The annoyance gravitated toward anger.

"Maybe not, but it's true." It was hard to admit it, but as the words left her mouth, there was a peace that settled over her. Derek was her past, he wasn't her future.

"So..." He paused, and she could hear the squeak of his office chair. "What are you going to do? Just hide out in some cabin in the middle of nowhere and pretend that's real life?"

"I'm not hiding, I'm thinking. Consider it a vacation—"

"Thinking about what? How to blow up your life completely? Don't you think you've done enough?"

The bitterness in his tone stung, but it solidified her decision. This was who Derek became when things didn't go his way. He would attack those around him. She'd overlooked that for a while now, but no longer. "I've got to go."

"Maddie, wait—"

"Take care of yourself, Derek." She hung up before he could respond and immediately turned off her phone.

She moved away from the kitchen and went to the window seat. Staring out at the property, watching the fresh snow fall, she realized she'd done the right thing. It felt as though she was closing a door, and that was never easy, even when it wasn't the right fit.

A movement near the main house caught her attention, and she found Nico and Oakley outside, building a snowman. Actually, Oakley seemed to be directing Nico, who was doing all the heavy lifting. Even from a distance, Maddie could see the little girl's animated gestures, and faint echoes of her orders were carried on the wind.

Nico rolled a massive snowball with effortless strength, positioning it carefully where Oakley pointed. When he did, she came closer and inspected her father's work before nodding.

As Maddie watched, Oakley turned and spotted her in the window. The little girl's face lit up with a smile, and she waved both arms, jumping up and down.

As she laughed, Maddie waved back.

Nico looked over, and for a moment, their gazes met across the distance. He didn't wave or even smile. Just looked at her with that intense, unreadable expression that made her pulse quicken. Then he gave a single, curt nod and turned back to building a snowman.

She stepped back from the window, her heart beating faster than it should. There was something about him and their interactions she couldn't put her finger on. An intensity that she wanted to explore.

By the time night fell, Maddie was restless and on edge. The day had dragged, and she had been unable to focus. The job search was still going nowhere. More rejection letters than anything. It should have bothered her, but she was hoping it was only a slight bump in the road to better things.

She'd just settled onto the sofa with a book when she heard movement outside. Heavy footballs crunching in the snow, and it sounded as though they were circling the cabin. She sat there frozen, every muscle tense.

Something large brushed against the side of the cabin, and a low rumbling sound echoed through the air. The hair on the back of her neck raised.

Stay inside after dark.

She stayed on the sofa, straining to track the sounds as whatever moved around the cabin's perimeter. But it was impossible. She tossed the book aside and, against every instinct, crept to the window.

Through the lacy curtain, she could see the nearly full moon, casting everything in silver light. At first, she saw nothing unusual, just trees and snow. Then the shadows shifted, and a massive shape emerged from the tree line. Too big to be a wolf or any normal animal.

It moved with fluid grace on four legs, its fur so dark it was almost black. But the eyes glowed amber in the moonlight.

Bears. Her breath caught as she pressed closer to the window.

Another shape joined the first, but this one was lighter in color. But before she could get a good look, another shape joined them, and then another.

Four large animals moving through the snow with purpose. They weren't hunting, at least not in the way predators typically hunted. They were...patrolling.

We'll set up patrols. We'll double them if we must.

The large black one stopped and turned its massive head toward her window. Even through the glass, she could feel the weight of its gaze. But what stole her breath were those amber eyes. She knew those eyes. *No, that's impossible.*

The creature didn't move. Just stared at her cabin with an intelligence that no animal should possess. She stumbled back from the glass, her thoughts racing.

"I'm seeing things." That had to be it. The stress and isolation were getting to her, making her see things that weren't there.

She forced herself to look again, to prove to herself it was all in her mind.

Instead of just trees and snow, she could see the creatures still there. They were moving away, disappearing into the woods. Within moments, they were gone, as if they'd never been there at all, but the tracks in the snow were all that remained.

She stood frozen by the window, listening to her own ragged breathing, and the overhead conversation ran through her thoughts. *My bear will deal with it.*

Her thoughts continued to spin. From the website again. *Some families carry the old blood.* To the amber eyes that glowed in the darkness and the way everyone in town had looked at her, assessing her. There were also Nico's cryptic warnings and the warmth of his body.

No, that's insane. Shifters aren't real. That's mythology or fantasy. It's impossible.

But she was certain of what she had seen. To prove it, she stepped back to the sofa and grabbed her laptop. With shaking hands, she opened the browser and typed: shapeshifter mythology.

Websites of indigenous legends and European folklore came up, but nothing concrete. She wanted proof but found nothing.

"Obviously. It's not like they'd want to advertise." She closed the laptop and set it aside before leaning back against the sofa.

She wanted a rational explanation. They were just normal bears. Extra-large, but normal bears. The eyes were just the same, but it wasn't actually Nico. Her eyes had been playing tricks on her.

"Or I'm losing my mind."

But deep down, she knew what she'd seen, and she knew those amber eyes.

CHAPTER 6

CHRISTMAS FESTIVAL

The next day, Maddie was in a fog of exhaustion and doubt. She told herself she'd imagined it or that it was a dream. Large bears, unusual lighting, and an overactive imagination fueled by stress had her hallucinating. Yet, every time she looked toward the main house and caught a glimpse of Nico moving through the snow with that predatory grace, her certainty wavered.

With her cell phone off, Derek had taken to emailing her repeatedly.

I'm sorry about what I said. Can we please talk?

Come on, Maddie, don't shut me out. Call me.

At least tell me when you're coming home.

Each email contained only a single line, but there were numerous. Each one she moved to the trash, without replying. She didn't respond, not because she was still angry, but because she didn't know what to say. Home...that wasn't her home anymore, it was Derek's apartment. Reminding her again that she had no plan and that her resources were dwindling.

"What am I going to do?" she mumbled to herself when, through the window, she caught a glimpse of Oakley headed toward the cabin.

Thankful for the distraction, Maddie opened the door to find the little girl practically bouncing with excitement, her cheeks flushed from the cold.

"Guess what, Miss Maddie? The Christmas festival starts tonight. The whole town does it every year, and there are lights, music, and hot chocolate." She barely paused for breath. "Will you come with us? Please? Daddy said I could ask you!"

Further up the path, Nico stood with his arms crossed. Even from a distance, Maddie could see his carefully neutral expression.

"A festival?" Despite her exhaustion, Maddie tried to match Oakley's enthusiasm.

"It's the best! They light the enormous Christmas tree in the square, and there's caroling. Mrs. Kate makes these amazing cookies, and there's a sledding hill. Oh, and there's going to be ice skating this year! They flooded the field to make the ice and everything. It's going to be so much fun." Oakley grabbed Maddie's hand. "Come on, Miss Maddie, you have to come."

She looked past Oakley to Nico, raising her eyebrow in question.

He strolled down the path, as if he were approaching something unpredictable. "The town holds an annual Christmas market and festival. It's a big deal around here. Oakley wanted to invite you."

"Just Oakley?" Maddie watched him, looking for any sign that he wanted her to join them.

Something flickered in his expression that she couldn't make out. "She's been talking about it nonstop since you braided her hair. I couldn't say no."

"But you would have preferred to?" A little disappointed, she watched him.

"I didn't say that." His jaw tightened.

"You didn't have to."

They stared at each other while Oakley looked between them, as if trying to decode the adult tension suddenly in the air around them.

"So, will you come? Please." Oakley pressed.

She looked down at the hopeful little face and felt her resistance crumble. The truth was, she desperately needed a distraction. Being around people, noise, and life would be better than sitting in the cabin, watching shadows, and questioning her sanity. Even if there was a possibility that the town residents were...bear shifters? The thought alone seemed absurd.

"I'd love to come." Afraid that she may see disappointment on Nico's face, she kept her attention on Oakley.

Oakley squealed and threw her arms around Maddie's waist. "This is going to be so much fun! You can meet Emma and see the tree lighting. Do you ice-skate? If you don't, Daddy can teach you. He's good. He taught me and Emma."

"Oakley," Nico said, his voice strained.

"What?" Oakley asked innocently.

"Don't worry, I can stake." Maddie met Nico's gaze over his daughter's head. "A little at least. It's been years since I went ice skating."

"We'll take it easy," he reassured her. "Oakley, let Miss Maddie go, she's got things to do."

"But—"

"No." Nico shook his head. "We need to get back, and I have work to do."

Oakley reluctantly released Maddie. "We'll come get you at four. Okay?"

"I'll be ready." She nodded.

As Oakley skipped back up the path, Nico lingered.

"You don't have to come." He glanced at her. "If you'd rather not—"

"I want to." She crossed her arms against the cold. "I mean, unless you don't want me there."

"It's not that."

"Then what is it?"

"The festive..." He paused as if trying to choose his words

carefully. "Everyone in town will be there. It can be overwhelming if you're not used to close-knit communities."

"I think I can handle it."

"Can you?" His amber eyes met hers. "You look exhausted, Maddie. Are you sleeping?"

"Such a way with words." She smirked. "I'm fine."

"That's not an answer."

"I've been having trouble sleeping. I think I'm just having trouble adjusting to the quiet. Guess I've been in the city too long."

"Just the quiet?" He raised an eyebrow at her, as if waiting for her to add something more.

She thought about the glowing eyes and massive bears moving through the darkness. But tried to keep that out of her tone. "What else would it be?"

He stepped close enough that she could feel the heat radiating from him despite the cold. "If something is bothering you, you can tell me."

"Can I?" She looked up at him, locking her gaze on his.

"Yes."

"Even if it sounds crazy?" Her voice was low, almost as if she didn't want him to hear it.

His expression shifted, and for a moment, she thought it was recognition in his gaze. "Especially then."

Maddie opened her mouth and then closed it. Unsure of what to even say. *I think I saw giant bears patrolling my cabin, and I think one of them might have been you.* Those words sounded crazy to her own ears, and she'd seen it. He'd think she'd lost her mind. *Maybe I have.*

"Nothing," she mumbled. "Just stress, I'm sure."

His gaze stayed locked on hers, clearly not convinced, but he didn't push either. "The offer stands. If you need to talk—"

"I know where you live."

The corners of his lips twitched, almost a smile.

"Daddy!" Oakley called from the path. "Come on! You said Miss Maddie is busy."

"I should go." But he didn't move away.

"Nico," she said softly. "Are you going to tell me what's really going on here?"

"What do you mean?"

"You know what I mean. The warnings, the cryptic comments, the way everyone in town looks at me like they're assessing if I'm a threat or—"

"You're not a threat." He cut her off before she could finish.

"What am I then?"

The question hung between them, heavy with implications neither of them seemed ready to address.

"Come to the festival. Meet the community and see for yourself what Timber Ridge is really like. Then maybe we can talk."

"About what?"

"Everything." He turned and walked away before she could respond. His long strides carried him up the path to where Oakley waited.

Maddie watched them go, her thoughts racing. *Then maybe we can talk...about everything.*

What was everything? The warnings? The strange sounds? The impossible things she believed she'd seen? Or something else entirely?

She stepped back inside and closed the door behind her. Her laptop, still sitting on the sofa, dinged with a new email.

"Probably another rejection email." Between the limited opportunities due to the season and her own hesitation about her future, the job hunt was going nowhere fast.

She dropped onto the sofa and grabbed her laptop. As the screen lit up, she saw three new emails. Two were from Derek.

This is ridiculous, Maddie. Call me.

Fine. Be that way.

While the one between those from Derek's was a reminder that rent was due in two weeks. Rent for the apartment she didn't have anymore. It was Derek's apartment now. She had the cabin she'd paid for through Christmas and nowhere to go after that. The rest of her belongings had been moved to a storage unit before she left town.

She deleted the emails and closed the laptop. The walls felt like they were closing in. She couldn't keep drifting like this. She needed a plan and to figure out what she was doing with her life, where she was going, and what she truly wanted.

Every time she envisioned the future, all she saw was a little girl with dark braids and an infectious smile. A man with amber eyes and secrets. A small mountain town that seemed to hum with hidden currents. Maybe she was trying to romanticize her escape, but it felt real.

Maddie glanced at herself in the mirror again, wondering if she should change again. Nothing she tried on seemed perfect. In the end, she'd settled on a forest green sweater that brought out her eyes and black jeans. She'd convinced herself that the festival would help. She'd see that Timber Ridge was just a quirky small town with people living their normal lives, nothing more. It would bring her perspective and maybe even a decent night's sleep.

At the clock struck four o'clock, Oakley knocked on the door.

She opened the door, and before she could say anything, Oakley bounced with joy.

"You look so pretty. Doesn't she look pretty, Daddy?" She glanced back at her father.

Nico stood behind his daughter, looking like he'd rather be anywhere else. But his gaze swept over Maddie, and she saw a flicker of appreciation and maybe even heat within his amber eyes before he quickly suppressed it.

"You look nice," he said, his voice neutral.

"So do you." She took in his dark jeans, a charcoal sweater that emphasized his broad shoulders, though the heavy coat hid most of his body from view. He'd shaved, his dark hair was slightly damp, and he smelled like pine and allspice, making her want to lean closer.

"Come on!" Oakley grabbed her hand and pulled her out of the doorway. "We're going to be late for the tree lighting."

She pulled the door shut behind her as they walked toward Nico's truck. It was a large, practical vehicle that somehow suited him perfectly. Nico opened the passenger door for her while Oakley scrambled into the back seat, chattering about all that the festival offered, but most of it passed over Maddie without a second thought. With her attention solely focused on Nico.

"Thank you for coming. It means a lot to her," Nico said as Maddie climbed in.

"Just to her?"

Without answering, his hand tightened on the door frame. "Try not to overthink everything. Just have a good time."

"Is that advice or a warning?"

"Both, probably." His lip curled up into a smirk.

Even with his warning, she pushed aside whatever weirdness existed in Timber Ridge. Right then, she was just a woman, headed to a Christmas festival with a father and daughter who had become important to her in the short time she'd been there. In that moment, it felt perfect, and she could handle that.

CHAPTER 7
FESTIVAL MAGIC

Timber Ridge had transformed into a winter wonderland. White lights were strung around the lampposts and wrapped around every tree on Main Street. Storefronts were decorated with evergreen garland, lights, and red ribbon. But nothing compared to the massive Christmas tree in the town square, which had to be at least thirty feet tall, stood waiting for the lighting ceremony. She'd seen it when she came to the market, but now it was decorated with ornaments that glittered in the last rays of the sun. The tree and town, all decked out, were impressive.

The air smelled of gingerbread, pine, and woodsmoke, while Christmas music drifted from speakers hidden among the decorations. People filled the streets, laughing and talking, creating the perfect atmosphere.

"Wow." Maddie stepped out of the truck and joined Nico and Oakley on the sidewalk.

"It's pretty great, right?" Oakley grinned up at her. "Just wait until you see it all lit up. That's always my favorite part. There's also a snowflake toss and a reindeer maze that you've got to try. It's so much fun."

As they walked toward the square, Maddie noticed people kept looking their way. Not so much the three of them, mostly just looking at her. Not every glance was suspicious, some were curious, and there was one woman who nodded at her in approval. It was all very confusing.

Nico's earlier words echoed within her thoughts: *Try not to overthink everything. Just have a good time.*

"Nico!" An older man with a silver beard waved at them from a booth selling handmade ornaments. "Glad you made it. This must be your guest!"

"Miss Garret is renting the cabin." Nico's hand settled on the small of her back, protective and possessive, as he led them closer to the booth. "Maddie, this is Thomas Reeves, Timber Ridge's mayor."

"Welcome to Timber Ridge." Thomas took her hand in a firm handshake. His eyes were a striking pale gray, but when he smiled, she could have sworn she saw them catch the light in an odd way. "Any friend of Nico's is welcome here."

"I'm—" Maddie started, but Oakley was already pulling her away.

"Come on, Miss Maddie, you have to meet Emma!"

For over an hour, Maddie had been swept into a whirlwind of introductions. It started with Emma, Oakley's best friend, and grew from there until she lost track of the names. Grayson, whom she met in the woods, was much friendlier in town than when he was on patrol. There was also a woman named Sarah who ran the bakery, and her gingerbread was divine.

Everyone was welcoming and warm, but there was something off about every encounter. Though it wasn't something Maddie could put her finger on. Maybe it was the way they moved—too graceful and fluid. Or the intensity in their eyes when they looked at her, as if assessing her. Or the way they all seemed to look to Nico, acknowledging him with a nod that felt formal. The town seemed to consider him more than a Christmas tree farmer or resident, but what that was, she wasn't certain.

"Hot chocolate!" Oakley announced, dragging Maddie toward a booth where Kate was serving mugs topped with whipped cream.

"Maddie." Kate smiled as she neared. "I'm glad you came. With Nico and Oakley as well."

"Oakley invited me. Said I couldn't miss it."

"Of course she did." Kate handed each of them a mug of hot chocolate. "That girl has great instincts."

"Thanks, Kate." Nico stepped closer to her until she could feel his warmth through their winter coats.

"Anytime, dear. You *three* have fun."

She raised an eyebrow at Kate, with the way she stressed *three*. It seemed as though she expected something more to develop.

As they sipped their hot chocolate, Oakley spotted Emma by the sledding hill and took off running, calling back. "I'll be back! Don't go anywhere."

Leaving Maddie alone with Nico in the middle of the crowded festival.

"She has a lot of energy." Maddie watched Oakley and Emma immediately start up the sledding hill.

"Always." Nico nodded. "Elena used to say she got it from my side of the family, but I always tried to argue."

"Your wife?"

"Yes." He sipped his hot chocolate. "Elena was quiet and thoughtful. She balanced me out. Oakley got my energy, but her mother's heart."

This was the first time she spoke about his late wife, and the grief was etched in the lines around his eyes. "How long has it been?"

"Four years." He swallowed hard. "She got sick...it happened so fast. One day she was fine and the next..."

"I'm sorry."

"Oakley barely remembers her. Sometimes that feels like a blessing, while other times it feels like another loss." He looked at her. "What about you? Your ex...you said you broke up recently?"

"About a month ago. It happened right after I lost my job." She let out a soft laugh that came out more bitter than anything. "Merry Christmas to me."

"It's rough timing."

"Corporate was downsizing, so it was just a wrong place, wrong time situation. But with Derek..." Her gaze focused on Oakley and Emma sledding down the hill, laughing like they were having the best time. "I think we'd been over for a while, but neither of us admitted it yet."

"Were you together long?"

"Four years. We lived together for almost two years. Part of me thought it was going somewhere. You know, marriage, kids, the whole thing. But really, it was just comfortable, and when things got difficult, he bailed." At first, she was angry, disappointed, and filled with emotions she couldn't name, but now she realized it was for the best.

"His loss."

The conviction in Nico's voice made her glance toward him. He was still focused on Oakley, but in his expression was a protectiveness.

"Now, I keep getting rejection emails from jobs I'm not even sure I want." The words were out before Maddie could think them through, surprising her. "I have no apartment, no plan, and no idea what I'm supposed to be doing. I came here to figure it out, but I'm..."

"Spiraling?" he supplied.

"Yes, spiraling. Is it that obvious?"

"I've been there, and you have that look like you're waiting for the next bad thing to happen."

She let out a chuckle. "Aren't you supposed to tell me everything is going to be fine?"

He turned toward her. "Would you believe if I did?"

"Probably not." Her lips curled into a smirk.

He smiled at her. The first genuine smile she'd seen from him, not the careful half-version he'd given her before. This smile transformed his face, making him look younger and approachable.

"I won't insult your intelligence. Life is messy, and sometimes it falls apart, but it doesn't mean you can't put it back together."

"Sounds like you're speaking from experience." Her gaze scanned his face, waiting to see if he gave anything away.

"Four years of it." The intensity in his gaze made her breath catch. "I thought I'd never feel normal again after Elena died. All this time, I've been going through the motions for Oakley's sake, but slowly things got better." He stepped closer. "Now, I'm starting to think different isn't a bad thing."

The charged moment stretched between them, and she was acutely aware of how close he was.

"Daddy! Miss Maddie!" Oakley cut off his words and shattered the moment. "Come sled with us!"

"Guess that's our cue." He stepped back, but his gaze stayed on her a moment longer.

"Miss Maddie, ride with me. We'll race, Daddy," Oakley hollered as they neared.

"Only if we win." She took the sled from Oakley and headed up the hill with Nico hot on their tails.

They spent the next hour sledding. Maddie and Oakley were on one sled while Nico was on another. Racing down the hill and trudging back up, breathless with laughter. Maddie couldn't remember the last time she'd felt so carelessly happy.

"It's time," Oakley hollered.

"For what?" Maddie asked as she brushed the snow from her pants.

"To light the tree," Nico explained as Oakley hurried ahead of them.

As the sun began to set, the town gathered in the square for the tree-lighting ceremony. Oakley climbed onto Nico's shoulders for a better view, and Maddie stood beside them, close enough that their shoulders brushed.

Thomas Reeves stood on the platform next to the tree. "Welcome, everyone, to our annual Festival of Lights! For generations, our families have gathered here to celebrate..."

As Mayer Reeves continued, Maddie's thoughts focused on his phrasing. It felt deliberate. *For generations. Our families.*

"We honor those who came before us and protect these mountains and the people who call them home. Those who carry the old ways forward."

The old ways. Maddie's pulse quickened.

"We welcome those who find their way to us, either by fate or chance."

Several residents glance toward her, and Nico tenses beside her. *What was that all about?*

"As we light this tree, we remember that we're stronger together. We protect our own, and we embrace those meant to be part of our circle."

As the ceremony continued in typical fashion with carols, a countdown, and the lighting of the tree, Maddie's thoughts kept circling back to the words Thomas had said. There seemed to be layers of meaning in every word, yet she couldn't quite grasp it.

When the tree blazed to life, the crowd cheered. The lights were beautiful, but in that moment, something else caught her attention. As the town residents turned their faces toward the illuminated evergreen, she saw it. The way their eyes catch the light, reflecting it back with an amber glow. Not everyone, but enough. Scattered throughout the crowd was a distinctive shine that no human eye should have. Her chest tightened as her breath caught.

Nico's hand found her elbow. "Maddie?"

Her gaze left the crowd to find him. In the white lights of the tree, his eyes were unmistakably amber. The lights reflected just like the creatures she'd seen in the woods.

"I..." Her voice came out strangled. "I need some air."

"You're outside, there's plenty of air right here."

"Less crowded air." With her heart racing, she backed away.

Nico lifted Oakley off his shoulders and glanced toward Grayson, who nodded before he followed Maddie as she pushed her way through the crowd toward a quieter side street.

She stopped next to a closed storefront and pressed her back against the cold brick as she focused on her breathing.

"Maddie." Nico came to stand in front of her, a careful distance away, with his hands in plain sight as if he was approaching a spooked animal. "Talk to me, Maddie. What's wrong?"

"Your eyes," she whispered.

"What?" The confusion was clear in his tone.

"Your eyes, they reflect light. Like..." She couldn't bring herself to say it. It was impossible.

"Maddie—"

"I saw them. That night. The shapes in the wood. They all had eyes like yours. Amber eyes that glowed." The words tumbled out of her. "A lot of those here have that reflection. The way you all move, the strength and heat—"

"Maddie." He stepped closer. "Stop."

"I'm not crazy." She stared up at him with wide eyes.

"I know."

"Then tell me I'm wrong. Tell me I'm seeing things. Because this can't be..."

He closed his eyes briefly, and when he opened them, she could see the conflict within them. "I can't tell you that."

"Because it's true?" Her words were barely audible as the world seemed to tilt.

"Because..." He turned back to the square where the carols and laughter continued. "Because, Maddie, there are things about this town and the people who call Timber Ridge home that I can't explain in the middle of a Christmas festival."

"But you can explain it?" She raised an eyebrow at him, uncertain.

"Yes."

"Would I believe you?"

His gaze met hers, and the raw honesty in his expression made her chest ache. "I don't know, but I think part of you already knows what's happening here."

She thought about the blog post, the overheard conversation, and the impossible grace and strength she'd witnessed. Some families carry the old blood.

"Shifters," she breathed. "You're all shifters. Bear shifters."

He didn't confirm or deny it, but he didn't have to. She saw the truth in his face and the way his shoulders dropped, as if a weight had been lifted.

"Oakley?" she asked.

"She will be. Right now, she's too young. It doesn't manifest until puberty."

"And you're what? The leader?" The way the town seemed to defer to him all started to make sense now.

"Something like that."

She sank down onto the cold ground, her head spinning. "This is insane."

He crouched in front of her but didn't touch her, just close enough that she could feel the warmth radiating off his body. "I know this is a lot. But, Maddie, you can't tell anyone. The safety of everyone here depends on secrecy."

"Who would I tell? Better yet, who would even believe me?"

"Your ex. Your family or friends."

She stared at him. This man, who'd been equal parts infuriating and intriguing since she met him, was apparently not entirely human. "I need time. To process this."

"I know, but Oakley is waiting, and if we don't go back, people will notice. Can you..." He hesitated. "Can you pretend everything's normal? Just for tonight?"

Could she stand in the town square surrounded by bear shifters and act like she hadn't just had her entire understanding of reality shattered? As she thought of Oakley, she nodded.

"For Oakley, but tomorrow—"

"Tomorrow, I'll tell you everything. I promise." He offered his hand, and after a moment, she took it, letting him pull her to her feet. His hand was warm and solid.

Even if he was a bear shifter, he was still Nico. Still, the man who braided his daughter's hair and brought firewood to her cabin, and that had to count for something.

As they walked back to the square together, Nico's hand stayed on her back. Though she wasn't sure if he meant to steady her or keep her from bolting.

"Daddy!" Oakley called as they neared the others, though her gaze quickly moved over to Maddie. "Miss Maddie, you've got to come to the cookie decorating booth. They always have the best cookies, and we can decorate them anyway we want."

Maddie's gaze focused on Oakley. Even with the information she learned, nothing changed in her mind. Oakley might one day transform into a bear, but the sweet girl already had Maddie wrapped around her finger. With a smile, she nodded. "Lead the way. If you say they're good, then we must try these cookies."

The silence in the truck was heavy with unspoken words, but Maddie didn't press as Nico drove them home. Oakley was asleep in the backseat, her head pressed against the window, while she clung to the stuffed gingerbread man they'd won at the snowflake-throwing booth.

"Tomorrow," he said as he pulled in front of the cabin. "We'll talk tomorrow."

"Promise?"

He nodded as he opened his door and got out. He was around the truck before she could open her door. "Promise."

He held out his hand, which she took, and he helped her down from the truck. He didn't say anything as he walked her to the door. As she opened it, he let go of her hand. "Good night, Maddie."

"Good night." She stepped inside, closed the door, and locked it. Yet she stood there by the window, watching as he got into the truck and drove up the hill to the main house. After several minutes, she spotted Nico's silhouette carrying Oakley inside.

Man. Father. Shifter. Yet somehow, despite everything, her heart still raced when he looked at her. She was either brave or the biggest fool. Only time would tell which.

CHAPTER 8
KISSING A BEAR

Maddie didn't sleep. She spent the night lying in bed, staring at the ceiling, while her mind replayed everything from the festival. The eyes. The words from the ceremony. Nico's face when she'd said the word "shifter" and he hadn't denied it.

Bear shifters. An entire town of them.

It should have terrified her, even sent her running back to the city, to normalcy. Instead, she kept thinking about Oakley and the young girl's laugh. Kate's warm smile. Even about how the whole community seemed to welcome her, not as an outsider joining them for a short time, but as someone who might belong. Most of all, she kept thinking of Nico.

By the time dawn broke, she'd convinced herself she was handling this remarkably well. At least she wasn't having a mental breakdown. Then, by her second cup of coffee, she was feeling almost normal.

Her phone buzzed with a text from an unknown number.

> Oakley's with my cousin Sarah today. If you're up for it, I could come by this morning. We should talk. – Nico

She stared at the message for a moment before replying, her hands shaking.

> Okay. When?

> Thirty minutes? His response comes almost immediately.

> I'll be here.

The last thing her nerves needed was more coffee. Still, she tried to busy herself brewing another pot. Her unanswered questions fluttered through her thoughts. How does shifting work? Has his family always been shifters? Can he control it, or did he just randomly find himself in bear form? Were they all bears, or were there other kinds of shifters?

When the knock finally came, she jumped despite expecting it.

"Okay, I'm a little jumpy still," she mumbled to herself as she walked over to the door.

Nico stood on her porch, looking as exhausted as she felt. Dark circles shadowed his eyes, and his hair looked as though he'd been running his hands through it.

"Hi," he said.

"Hi."

They stared at each other for a long moment, neither of them moving.

"Can I come in?" he asked.

"Sorry, yes, come in." She stepped back, allowing him to enter the cabin. As he did, the scent of pine, woodsmoke, and spice that was all him drifted past her.

Inside, he shrugged off his coat but didn't move further into the cabin, as if he wasn't sure if she wanted him in her space.

"Coffee?" she offered, moving away from the door.

"Sure." He hung his coat on the hook by the door before following her.

In the kitchen, she poured him a mug, grateful for something to do with her hands. Then, she turned back to find him standing near the kitchen bar, watching her with an intensity that made her pulse quicken.

"So, bear shifters?" She set the mug on the bar in front of him.

"Yeah." Without taking his attention off her, he wrapped his large hand around the mug of coffee.

"That's all you're going to say?"

"I don't know where to start." He lifted the mug of coffee but didn't bring it to his lips. "What do you want to know?"

"Everything. Nothing. I don't know." She let out a soft chuckle. "How about we start with the basics? You can actually turn into a bear?"

He nodded.

"A full bear? Not just partially?" She wasn't even sure what she thought partially turning into a bear would look like, but it seemed like a logical question at the moment.

"Full transformation. Though we can do partial shifts if we wish. Claws, teeth, and enhanced strength. Whatever we need. But a full shift is a complete change," he explained.

"Same with everyone in town?"

"Not everyone." He took a sip of his coffee. "Maybe three-quarters, the rest are human, married in or born to mixed couples. They obviously know what we are, as it's too hard to hide something like this in a small community."

"Oakley?"

"She'll be able to shift around twelve or thirteen. To be a shifter... well, it's genetic. You can't be bitten like some movies make out. Elena and I carried the gene, so Oakley will definitely shift. With mixed couples, you have to wait until puberty to be certain, though there are usually some signs before that."

The information was overwhelming as Maddie tried to process it. "But...that night I heard sounds outside. That was you, wasn't it? Patrolling?"

He nodded. "There's a young shifter, not from our clan, who has been hunting on our territory. We've been tracking him, trying to figure out if he's a threat or just a lone shifter lost. I'm sorry if we scared you."

"You did, but now it makes perfect sense that you kept telling me to stay inside after dark. I—"

"We would never hurt you, Maddie. None of us. But I couldn't explain without...well, without all of this."

"Why didn't you just tell me to leave? Wouldn't that have been easier?"

His lips cocked up into a cocky smile as his eyes sparkled with amusement. "I tried. Remember? The first night. You wouldn't go, and then Oakley met you and..."

"And what?" she pressed when he trailed off.

"And my bear didn't want you to leave."

The words hung in the air for a long moment.

"Your bear," she repeated. Not so much a question, but a statement.

"It's hard to explain. My bear is part of me, but also separate. It has its own instincts and desires." His gaze met hers. "The moment you opened that door, it recognized you."

"Recognized me as what?"

"It's complicated." Though the look in his eyes made her think he wanted to say something else.

"Nico, everything about this is complicated."

"I know, and I'm sorry." He let out a deep breath. "I never meant for you to get caught up in all this. You were supposed to have peace and quiet here, instead, you got..."

"Got what?" she pressed.

"A shifter town with secrets." He laughed humorlessly.

Without comment, she moved to the window and looked out at

the snow-covered landscape. Everything looked the same as it had every day since she arrived, yet everything was different. "I should be terrified. Instead of standing here talking to you, I should be packing my things to leave. But I'm not. Why is that?"

"Only you can answer that."

She turned to face him. "Do you want me to leave?"

"No." His voice was raised, and his eyes widened as if he didn't like the idea. "No, Maddie, I don't want you to leave. But maybe you should anyway. For your own safety and peace of mind."

"What if I don't want peace of mind? What if I want..." She let her words fade off, unsure how to finish them.

Nico stepped around the counter, coming to join her at the window. "What do you want, Maddie?"

You. This is crazy because you're a bear shifter and I've known you for less than two weeks. This whole thing is impossible.

"I want answers," she forced herself to say instead. "I want to understand."

Over the next hour, Maddie learned more about shifters than she could wrap her brain around. Nico explained everything from shifter history to clan structure and the importance of territory. His family had been in these mountains for generations. He even tried to explain how shifting worked. First, there was pain, but the freedom he experienced made everything worth it. Connecting with his bear instincts heightened his senses and strength. All of it allowed him to look at traditional bears in a whole new light.

She learned more about Elena and their mating bond. When she died, it nearly destroyed him. Raising Oakley alone, trying to be both parents, was what held him together. Now he was trying to balance teaching her about her heritage while still protecting her childhood.

Everything he said helped her better understand him. This wasn't a movie, these were real people with lives and families, and hopes and fears.

"What about your sister, Lucia, is she...?"

"A shifter? Yes, but she never wanted this life. As soon as she was old enough, she left Timber Ridge behind and rarely comes home to visit." Pain clouded his amber eyes. "I didn't handle it well. Even now, things are bumpy between us. I tend to control things rather than understand what she needed. That's why she rented you the cabin without asking. She was trying to make a point."

"A point to show you that you don't get to control everything?"

"Yeah." He smiled ruefully. "She's right, but that's my job. It's a protective instinct, which might have gone overboard."

"Because you lost Elena."

"Because I couldn't protect Elena. She got sick, and all my strength and my bear's power, yet none of it mattered. I couldn't save it. So now I try to protect everyone else. I want to keep everyone safe. Keep them close. It's exhausting, and now Oakley's starting to push back against my control. I know I need to let go, but—"

"But you're scared."

"Terrified," he admitted.

Without thinking, she stepped closer, drawn by the vulnerability in his voice. "For what it's worth, you're doing an amazing job with Oakley. She's happy, healthy, and full of love. That's because of you."

"All because of my cousins, my aunts, heck, half the town helped raise her."

"But mostly, you. I see it in the way she looks at you."

They were standing close enough that Maddie could feel the heat radiating from him, and she could see the gold flecks in his eyes. She could almost feel his bear below the surface.

"Oakley will be home soon. I should probably go," Nico said, but didn't step back.

"Okay."

"And we should..." His words trailed off. "We need to set some boundaries. About this. About us."

"What *us*?" Her voice came out breathier than intended.

"That's the problem. There shouldn't be an *us*. You're human, and you're leaving in a week. You just found out about shifters, which makes this the worst possible timing for..." He gestured between them.

"For what?" she pressed when he went silent.

"For the way I feel about you."

Her breath caught. "How do you feel about me?"

"Like I'm standing on the edge of a cliff. If I take one more step, I'm falling. Like my bear is about to do something stupid and claim you as—" he cut himself off, jaw clenched as if to stop the words from flowing freely.

"As what?"

"Doesn't matter." He shook his head.

"It matters to me." For a long moment, their gazes stayed locked, tension crackling in the air between them.

"I should go," he said again.

"Then stop saying that and just go." She let out a deep breath.

"I can't when you're looking at me like that."

"Like what?" It came out breathier than she meant.

"Like you want me to kiss you." He stepped closer.

"Maybe I do."

Nico made a low, growly sound in his throat. "Maddie—"

"If you don't want this, just say so. Stop pretending you're leaving when we both know you want to stay."

"It's not about wanting, it's about what's smart and safe—"

"I'm tired of playing life safe." She moved closer, close enough to feel his breath on her face. "I want to know what it feels like. This thing between us. I want to stop pretending it doesn't exist."

"Once we start this, I don't know if I can stop." The honesty in his words hit her full force, but she didn't back away.

"Then don't."

Those two words were all it took to shatter Nico's control. He closed the rest of the distance separating them, and his hand cupped the back of her neck, drawing her closer as his lips claimed hers like a man drowning.

Maddie gasped against his mouth, and he took advantage, deepening the kiss with a hunger that made her knees weak. She grabbed his shoulders for balance and felt nothing but solid muscle and barely restrained power.

Under her touch, he felt warm. Not feverishly hot but radiating heat like a furnace. The scent of him hit her full force. He smelled of pine and snow, and something else she couldn't quite put her finger on, but wild, and it made her want to press closer to him.

He backed her toward the door, his body covering hers, while one hand tangled in her hair, and the other gripped her hip. The kiss was consuming, demanding, and like nothing she had ever experienced before.

When he finally pulled back, they were both breathing hard. His eyes were fully glowing now.

"Maddie." His voice was rougher, deeper than before. "I have to stop."

"Why?" She pulled him back down, kissing him again.

He groaned against her lips, his control visibly fraying. His fingers tightened on her, and she felt something sharp. *Claws.* The realization should have terrified her, but it sent a thrill through her body.

But the fact that his claws were out seemed to snap him back to reality. He wrenched himself away, stumbling backward, his chest heaving. "I can't...I can't control it when you're this close."

"Control what?"

"My bear, it wants..." He dragged his hand through his hair, and she saw his fingers were tipped with dark claws. "It wants to claim you. To mark you as mine. But I can't let that happen."

"Why?"

"Because you don't understand what that means. Because you're human and Maddie, you're leaving." The reasons flooded forward as he backed toward the door. "I'm sorry. I shouldn't have touched you. This was a mistake."

"Nico—"

But he pulled open the door and was already making his way out, shifting mid-strike. One moment, he was a man, the next, a massive bear crashing through the snow toward the tree line.

She stood in the doorway, her body still tingling from his kiss and want, as she watched him disappear into the woods. She touched her lips, still feeling the ghost of his kiss. Still feeling the press of claws against her skin and the heat of his body pressed against hers.

She just kissed a bear shifter who told her this was a mistake. Yet all she could think was that she wanted him to come back and make that same mistake again and again.

CHAPTER 9
WARM COOKIES,
COLD DISTANCE

For three days, Maddie watched the main house from her window, catching glimpses of Nico working around the property, chopping wood, checking fences, and loading supplies into his truck. But he never looked toward the cabin. He never came down the path.

He's avoiding me.

She tried to convince herself it was for the best. The kiss had been intense and dangerous in ways she was still processing. He was a bear shifter with a daughter, and he was still in love with his dead wife. That wasn't the only problem. She was an unemployed mess with little idea of what she was doing with her life.

This is why we should stop anything more from happening.

Even knowing that, she kept touching her lips, remembering the heat of his mouth on hers. She stood at the window like a lovesick teenager, hoping to catch a glimpse of him.

By midday, she was going crazy from being stuck inside when a knock echoed through the cabin, and her heart leaped. *Nico.* Hopeful that it was him, she set the book she was reading aside and got up from the sofa.

KELSEY KARSON

Opening the door, she found not Nico, but Oakley, bundled in her pink coat with a mischievous smile on her face.

"Miss Maddie, can I come in?"

"Does your dad know you're here?" Maddie asked, even as she stepped aside to let the young girl in.

"He's busy fixing the fence on the north side." Oakley shrugged off her coat. "I brought cookie cutters. I thought maybe we could make Christmas cookies? Daddy's been too busy, and I really want to make some."

"Okay, but we're going to do this properly. I'm going to text your dad, so he knows where you are."

"You have his number?"

She grabbed her cell phone from the counter, where it had sat for days, untouched. The battery was low, but it didn't matter because when she opened her text messages, she realized she'd deleted his earlier text, and he hadn't texted since.

"I guess I don't."

"Don't worry, Miss Maddie, he'll figure it out. He always knows where I am anyway."

What does that mean? Can shifters track their family members? Can he track everyone? The thoughts circled through her mind, but Oakley's flurry of movements brought her back to the present.

"Do you have everything we need for cookies? If not, I can raid our pantry." Oakley asked, pulling open the refrigerator.

"I sure do. It's not Christmas if you don't make cookies." She smiled at Oakley as she set her cell phone on the counter and opened the cabinet with the dry ingredients she had purchased at the market in town, intending to make cookies herself.

They spent the next hour baking, or rather, making a spectacular mess. With Oakley's enthusiastic baking ways, flour ended up everywhere. But her laughter was infectious, and Maddie found herself relaxing for the first time in days.

"These are going to be the best cookies ever," Oakley announced, carefully cutting out a tree shape from the dough. "Even better than the ones Daddy and I make."

"I don't know about that. Those were pretty amazing cookies."

"These are special, though, because I made them with you." Oakley glanced up at Maddie. "I like having you here, Miss Maddie. It feels like..."

"Like what?" She pressed.

"Like having a family." Oakley's voice was soft, and Maddie's throat tightened.

"I like being here too, sweetie."

"Are you gonna stay after Christmas?" Oakley asked, putting the tree-shaped cookie on the baking sheet.

"I don't know. Lucia only rented me the cabin through the holidays, so it's up after the New Year."

"But you could stay longer! Aunt Lucia never comes back anyway, and Daddy owns the cabin. I know he'd let you stay!"

"It's complicated." How was she supposed to explain it to a six-year-old when she wasn't even sure she understood it herself?

"Grown-ups always say things are complicated, but usually they're just being stubborn." She grabbed the star cookie cutter and began to cut another cookie. "Like Daddy's being weird lately. All grumpy and distracted. I think it's because of you. He keeps looking toward the cabin."

"Oakley—"

"It's in a good way!" Oakley cut her off. "He's been sad since Mama died. He smiled before you came, but it wasn't real. There was no spark in his eyes like now. But something happened, and it's sad again. Did you guys fight?"

"Not exactly. It's...complicated."

"There's that word again." With a huff, Oakley rolled her eyes with an impressive six-year-old attitude. "Do you have a boyfriend, Miss Maddie?"

"Uh..." The question caught Maddie off guard. "No."

"Good."

"Oakley." Even as her lips curled into a smile, she couldn't help but scold.

"What? It's good. If you had a boyfriend, you couldn't date my daddy." Oakley looked up at Maddie before adding. "I think you should date Daddy."

With her mouth slightly open, she didn't know if she should laugh or cry. "That's very sweet, but—"

"He needs a girlfriend. Being alone isn't healthy."

"Where did you hear that?"

"Aunt Lucia." Oakley shrugged. "You're nice and pretty, and if you don't mind that our family is..."

"Different?" Maddie supplied.

The young girl's eyes widened. "You know?"

Maddie nodded. "Your dad told me about the shifting."

"Oh, really!" Oakley's face lit up. "He told you? That's huge. He never tells anyone. See, you are perfect for him. Since you know, does that mean you'll stay? Does that mean you and Daddy—"

"We're friends," Maddie said firmly, even though she wasn't sure that was all they were.

"But you kissed him."

"What?" Her hands shook as she slid the cookie sheet into the oven.

"I can smell it. I could smell your scent on him when he came home. That means you kissed, hugged, or something," Oakley stated matter-of-factly. "Shifters can smell stuff like that."

"That's...well, that's invasive."

"Well, I don't know what invasive means, but I can't help it. It's just like smelling the roses. But you kissed him, didn't you?"

"Oakley—"

"I won't tell anyone. It's a secret." She mimed zipping her lips. "But I'm happy about it. Daddy deserves to be happy, and so do you. I think you make each other happy."

Oh boy.

But at least Oakley dropped the subject as she began humming

Christmas carols, which gave Maddie a moment to process the six-year-old's romantic advice.

"I don't remember my mama very much," Oakley said softly. "Just little things. I remember her voice and that she smelled like vanilla. She used to braid my hair."

"Your dad braids your hair now."

"It's not the same. He tries but..." She picked at a spot of dried flour on the table. "Sometimes I wish I had a mama again. Someone who could teach me things, and I could talk to, like Emma has her mama."

Maddie's heart broke as she knelt to Oakley's level. "Your dad is doing an amazing job raising you. You know that, right?"

"I know, but he's not a mama, and I miss having one. I might not remember her, but I still miss her. When I look at Emma and her mama, it makes me miss it more."

"It's completely normal to want a mom, and it's okay to miss someone you barely remember." Maddie pulled her into a hug.

"Do you think Mama would have liked you?"

"I..." Caught off guard by the question, Maddie stumbled over her answer. "I don't know, sweetie."

"I think she would, and I think she'd be happy Daddy found someone who makes him happy again. Someone who is good to me, too." Oakley pulled back, wiping her eyes with the back of her hand. "Sorry."

"There's nothing to apologize for. You're being honest, and that Oakley is very brave."

"Well, let's brave the oven and decorate some cookies. I want to taste them." Oakley chuckled as she bounced up and down.

They ended up spending longer decorating each cookie than it had taken them to cut out the shapes. But every moment with Oakley was a joy. Nico was raising a charming little girl. Even as Oakley chattered on, Maddie's thoughts continued to circle back to Nico and his late wife. Would she approve? Would the shifters in town who thought so highly of Nico approve of her, or would her humanity be something they couldn't overlook?

Daddy deserves to be happy, and so do you.

That stuck with Maddie. Did she deserve to be happy? After the implosion of her life, didn't she deserve something good? Was Nico something good or another complication? Either way, it was a fresh start in more ways than one.

"Thank you, Miss Maddie." Oakley put on her coat to leave. "I had so much fun. I hope we can do this again before you leave."

"You're going to turn into a cookie if you keep eating them all." Maddie smiled as she held out a plate full of decorated cookies for Oakley to take home. "Share some with your dad."

"I'm making no promises." She smirked.

Before she could walk Oakley to the door, her phone buzzed on the counter.

Nico?

She grabbed the phone, and as her gaze fell on the screen, her hopes were dashed. Derek's name appeared with yet another text message.

I made a mistake. Can we talk? Please.

She stared at it, feeling nothing but a vague sense of exhaustion.

"Is that your ex?" Oakley stood next to her, glancing at the phone screen.

"Oakley!"

"Sorry, I can't help it." She glanced up at Maddie. "Are you gonna talk to him?"

"I don't know."

"Do you want to?" Oakley pressed.

A month ago, she would have said yes immediately. Would have jumped at the chance to fix things. But now the desire was gone. The normalcy she had with Derek felt like settling.

"No," Maddie admitted, more to herself than Oakley. "I don't think I do."

"Good, because you should be with my daddy instead." Oakley beamed. "He's better than some guy who sends sorry texts."

Maddie just stared at the young girl. She was far too smart for her own good.

"I'm taking these to Daddy. Maybe it will make him less grumpy." With cookies in hand, she skipped toward the door. "Bye, Miss Maddie."

Maddie followed her to the door and watched as Oakley made her way up the path toward the main house. When Oakley reached the porch, she turned back and waved at Maddie before disappearing inside.

Maddie stepped inside, shut the door, and headed to the sofa. Her cell phone was still in her hands as she debated what to say to Derek.

> I don't think there's anything to talk about. We're done. Please stop texting me.

His response came immediately.

> Maddie, don't do this. Whatever's going up there, it's not real. Come home. We can figure this out.

She wanted to tell him that she was home. Timber Ridge felt like home. But at the same time, it felt like an impossible situation.

> I need you to respect my decision. Goodbye, Derek.

Before he could respond, she deleted his number.

For a long moment, she sat there, feeling the weight of her decision. She had closed another door, burned another bridge. But instead of panic, she felt a sense of release.

She set down her phone and looked around the cabin. Christmas cookies cooled on the counter, and lights twinkled from where she had strung them around the window. The small, fake Christmas tree sat on the coffee table. It wasn't enough to really feel like she was celebrating, but for the first time, it felt like she was building a new life. It might be in a strange place, with secrets of its own, but it felt right.

"Sometimes you just have to be brave enough to choose what makes you happy. Even if what makes you happy could turn into a bear."

CHAPTER 10
THINGS HE WON'T SAY

The morning sunlight was an unexpected change from the gloomy, snowy days that had been routine since she had arrived at the cabin. Maddie stepped out onto the porch to gather firewood, but was greeted by brooding Nico instead.

"We need to talk."

Clutching a piece of wood that she'd gathered, she spun toward the voice. Only, instead of a threat, she found Nico coming around the side of her cabin. "You scared me."

"Inside." He tipped his head toward the door.

"Good morning to you, too."

Without moving toward the door, she took him in. He looked exhausted. Dark circles shadowed his eyes, and tension radiated from every line in his body. This wasn't a friendly visit. He was all business.

"Maddie, this is serious." He stepped onto the porch and paused near the door, waiting for her.

She grabbed a couple more logs from the firewood stack and headed inside. She didn't bother to glance behind her to see if he followed, she knew he was there. Instead, she crossed the short distance to the living room and placed the firewood in the basket in the hearth.

When she turned toward him, she found him standing near the kitchen island, his coat still on. He just stood there as if he were about to deliver bad news.

"What's wrong?"

"There's been more activity. The young shifter I mentioned before is getting bolder. We found fresh kills this morning, closer to the houses. One was less than a quarter mile from here. Bordering my property."

"Kills? Like animals?"

"Deer. Elk. He's hunting, but he's not careful about it. He doesn't cover his tracks. It's as if he wants us to notice." His jaw tightened. "Or he doesn't know better."

"Why would that make him dangerous?"

"Because a shifter who can't control himself, who hunts recklessly, who doesn't respect territory, is how shifters get exposed. It could lead to humans discovering us and panicking. Panic leads to us being hunted down like—" He stopped himself.

"Like animals." She finished for him.

"Yeah."

The sadness in that single word made her want to cross over to him and wrap her arms around him. Instead, she forced herself to go to the kitchen to make a pot of coffee. Anything to keep her hands busy.

"So why are you telling me?"

"You need to stay close to the cabin, especially after dark. No walks in the woods or exploring. If you need something from town, text me first. I'll have someone escort you."

"Escort me?" She spun toward him, anger flaring through her. "Like I'm a prisoner?"

"Like you're someone who could get hurt."

"By this other shifter?"

"By a situation you don't understand."

"Then explain it to me." She crossed her arms over her chest and stared at him. "You kiss me as if your life depended on it, then you disappear for days. Now you show up giving me orders like I'm one of your clan members who has to obey. Which is it, Nico? Am I someone you care about or just another problem you have to manage?"

His amber eyes flashed gold as he met her stare. "You think I don't care? You think I've been avoiding you because I don't want to be near you?"

"Honestly, Nico, I don't know what to think. You won't even talk to me."

"I'm trying to protect you," he growled.

"From what? This rogue shifter or yourself?"

His shoulders tensed, and she realized it was a direct hit.

"Both," he said tightly.

"Why?"

"Because you don't understand what you do to me or what being near you does to my control." He took a step closer. "My bear wants to claim you. Every time I see you, every time I catch a whiff of your scent, it takes everything I have not to—"

"Go on. Not to what, Nico?"

"Not to mark you as mine." His voice was rough and strained. "To bond with you in a way that can't be undone. I can't do that, Maddie. You're human, and you don't understand what a mating bond means or what it would cost you."

"Explain it to me." Her heart raced, but she needed to know.

"It's permanent, as in forever. You'd be tied to me, to this clan, and this life. You'd feel what I feel. You'd never be able to leave or choose anything different." He dragged his hand through his hair. "You deserve better than that. Maddie, you deserve a choice."

"What if I choose you?"

"You don't truly understand what that means."

"Then tell me. Tell me all the nitty details." She moved close, frustrated with this dance. "Stop protecting me and just tell me the truth. All of it. I deserve that much, Nico."

He closed his eyes, visibly wrestling with himself. When he looked at her again, gold pupils dilated with animalistic desire, and she realized his bear was closer to the surface. It was almost as if she could feel it pulsing within him and the air around him.

"A mating bond is sacred. When a shifter finds their true mate, it's instinctive and inevitable. In a relationship like this, the bear would know before the human." He looked at her, and the raw honesty in his expression made her breath catch. "My bear knew it the moment you opened that door. It recognized you as mine. I tried to send you away because I knew you were trouble. I should have demanded you leave before—"

"Before what?"

"Before I fell for you."

Her heart skipped a beat, and the words hung between them.

"Nico—"

"But it doesn't matter what I feel." He cut her off. "Bonding with you would change your life irrevocably. Being a shifter mate, you'd age more slowly. You'd be connected to me in ways you can't imagine. But most importantly, if something happened to me, it would destroy you the way Elena's death nearly destroyed me. I can't do that to you." His voice broke slightly.

"Don't I get a say in this?" She stepped closer until she was right in front of him. Close enough to touch, but she kept her hands at her side.

"You don't understand what you'd be agreeing to."

"You keep saying that." She let out a soft breath and met his gaze. "Nico, you have to stop making decisions for me and let me decide for myself. So tell me everything."

"I can't." The anguish was clear in his words. "Not yet, not when there's a rogue shifter in my territory. I need to focus on protecting my daughter and you. Just stay close to the cabin. Please. For me. Can you do that?" He backed toward the door.

"Nico, you're running again."

"I'm trying to keep you safe."

"By pushing me away?" Her eyebrows knitted in confusion.

"By not pulling you in deeper than you already are." He reached for the door handle. "There's a clan meeting tonight about the route. I have to be there, but I'll have Grayson patrolling the area and making sure you're secure."

"I don't need a babysitter," she snapped.

"Yes, you do. You just don't know it yet."

"I'm tired of you telling me what I know and don't know when you won't tell me the whole story."

"Maddie—"

"Just go, Nico." She was surprised at the steel in her voice. "You can't treat me like a child who can't make their own decisions."

"I'm trying to do the right thing," he argued.

"The right thing is trusting me and talking to me. Not running away when things get intense." She stepped around him and opened the door, letting the cold air whip through.

Nico stood there for another moment. She could read the struggle on his face. The man who wanted to stay, the alpha fighting to keep control, and the bear beneath it all, straining to claim her.

"I'm sorry, Maddie. I know I'm handling this badly. I just don't know how to do this. How to want someone, yet know it's wrong."

"It's not wrong." The conviction in her words startled her.

"It is when I can't give you what you deserve. I can't promise you safety, normalcy, or—"

"What if that isn't what I want? Maybe normal is overrated. What if I want this?" She gestured toward him. "Complicated, messy, and very real."

"You don't mean that."

"Stop telling me what I mean!" she snapped in annoyance.

"Maddie, can you honestly say you'd choose to become a shifter's mate? To be bound to someone forever? You'd be giving up any chance of a normal human life." His voice rose. "Because that is what you'd be choosing. There is no going back from this decision. No changing your mind once you understand the reality of the situation."

"My old life wasn't working. I was miserable," she admitted. "Why would I want to go back to that?"

"It was safe, and because it made sense."

"But that doesn't make me happy." She stared at him, the air between them crackling with tension.

Nico moved first, closing the distance in three strides and backing her against the door frame. His hands came up to frame her face, and his eyes were fully gold now. His bear was right there beneath the surface.

"You're making this impossible," he said, his voice rough.

"Good."

He leaned in, and for a moment, she thought he was going to kiss her again. Instead, he pressed his forehead against hers. "I can't. If I start now, I won't stop. I can't claim you like this. Not when you don't fully understand what it means. I promise I'll explain later. For now, just stay safe. Stay close to the cabin until I handle this rogue situation, and then we'll talk."

"Promise?"

"Promise." He stepped back, putting distance between them. "Grayson will be around. If you need anything, anything at all, call me. I'll come."

"I deleted your number."

He reached down and pulled his phone out of his pocket. Quickly typed out something, and she heard her phone vibrate across the room. "You have it now. Call me, and I'll come."

"Will you? Or will you send someone else?"

"I'll come." The certainty in his voice was reassuring.

Without another word, he strolled out the door that was still open, heading toward the main house. Maddie stood there and watched as he left. Frustration and confusion churn in her chest.

She understood what he was trying to do. Protect her and even give her space to make an informed decision. But this noble and self-sacrificing Nico was driving her crazy.

She stepped back and slammed the door harder than necessary.

Through the window, she watched as Nico stopped halfway up the path and looked back at the cabin. Even from a distance, she could see the longing in his posture. The way he swayed slightly, as if he was fighting the urge to come back. Then he turned and continued up the hill, disappearing into the main house.

Maddie grabbed one of the Christmas cookies from the kitchen counter and bit into it viciously, as if she could take her annoyance out on it. "Stupid noble bear shifter. Stupid mating bonds."

She grabbed her phone and looked down at the message.

> Call, and I'll always come.

The annoyance fell away as a smile curled up the corner of her lips.

In her hand, her phone buzzed. A text from an unknown number.

> This is Grayson. Nico asked me to check in. I'll be patrolling the area tonight. You won't see me, but I'll be close. Stay inside after dark.

"Great. Now I have a shifter bodyguard."

Another text popped onto the screen.

> I'm coming up there. We need to talk face-to-face. I'll be there in two days.

> No. There's nothing more to say. Don't contact me again.

She let out a deep sigh and blocked his number. Her mate, who kept bolting, a rogue shifter on the loose, and now her ex-boyfriend had decided to show up.

CHAPTER II
SOMEONE WHO STAYS

The next afternoon, Maddie was curled up on the sofa with one of the few books she had brought with her. Though it was difficult to focus on the plot, her thoughts ran wild. A small, urgent knock rattled her door. She set the book aside and tossed off the covers before heading to the door.

When she opened the door, she found Oakley standing there, her face blotchy and tear-streaked.

"Oakley, what's wrong?"

"Can I come in?" The girl's voice was thick with suppressed tears.

"Of course." Maddie pulled her inside and helped her out of her coat. "What happened, sweetie? Are you hurt?"

"No." Oakley wiped her nose on her sleeve. "I just...I heard Daddy on the phone. He was arguing with someone. He sounded really mad but also sad."

"Come sit down. I'll make you some hot chocolate. That always helps me when I'm sad."

Oakley settled on the sofa with a blanket while Maddie heated milk on the stove. She was making the real stuff, not instant, just as her mother always had. Hot chocolate made with love could fix almost anything.

"Do you know who he was talking to?" Maddie asked carefully.

"Aunt Lucia, I think. At least he said her name." Oakley pulled the blanket tighter around herself. "He was saying stuff like 'I need more notice, you can't just show up' and 'I can't deal with this right now, not with everything else.' Why was he so upset?" Fresh tears welled up in her eyes.

"Oh, sweetie."

"Am I the everything else? Am I making things hard for him?" Oakley's voice broke. "Because I heard him talking to Uncle Grayson the other day about how hard it is being a single dad. I know I'm a lot of work, but maybe if I were better behaved—"

"Stop. You're not making things hard for your dad." Maddie brought over two mugs of hot chocolate and sat beside Oakley on the sofa. "Here you go. I didn't make it too hot so that you could enjoy it now."

Oakley held the hot chocolate in her hands but didn't take a sip. Instead, she sat there, staring down at the miniature marshmallows decorating the top.

"Oakley, you're the best thing in his life. Do you understand?"

"But lately he's always stressed."

"Because he loves you so much, it scares him. He wants to do everything perfectly for you. Not because you're too much." Maddie tucked a stray hair behind Oakley's ear. "Your dad is dealing with a lot right now with work, family, and adult stuff. It has nothing to do with you. You're wonderful, Oakley."

"You really think so?" She sniffed and took a sip of hot chocolate.

"I'm positive."

"Miss Maddie?" Oakley glanced up at her, hot chocolate mustaches and all. "Do you think you'll stay? After Christmas, I mean."

"I don't know, sweetie. I don't really have a plan yet."

"But you could stay, right? If you wanted to?" The hope in Oakley's voice made Maddie's chest tighten.

"It's not that simple."

"Why? You said you don't have a job anymore. No boyfriend. And you like it here." Oakley set down her mug and turned toward Maddie. "I like having you here. And Daddy..."

"What about your daddy?"

"He's happier when you're around." Oakley's expression was far too knowing for a six-year-old. "He smiles more. Real smiles, not fake ones he does for others. He laughs. Before you arrived, I can't remember the last time he laughed."

"Oakley—" She started before the young girl cut her off.

"I can tell you like him, and I know he likes you too. So why can't you stay? We could be like a family. You, me, and Daddy. Doesn't that sound nice?"

If Maddie were honest with herself, it sounded wonderful. It sounded like everything she hadn't known she wanted until that moment. A little girl who needed her, a man who made her heart race, and a small mountain town full of secrets and warmth.

"It sounds nice...really nice," Maddie admitted softly.

"Then stay! Please! I don't want you to leave. I don't want things to go back to the way they were. I don't want—" Oakley's voice cracked. "I don't want to lose someone else."

"Oh, sweetie." Maddie pulled Oakley into her arms, feeling the girl shake as tears rolled down her face. "You're not going to lose me. Even if I leave, we can still talk. We can even video chat."

"It's not the same." Oakley's voice was muffled against Maddie's shoulder. "Nothing is ever the same when people leave. Aunt Lucia left. We used to talk all the time, but now she's too busy. Mama left, and she's never coming back. Everyone leaves."

The raw pain in her words tightened Maddie's chest. She held Oakley tighter, rocking her slightly like her own mother used to. "I'm sorry you've had to deal with so much loss."

"Then stay," Oakley pleaded.

How could she explain that it wasn't that simple? Staying meant navigating whatever complicated thing existed between her and Nico. It also means committing to a life she'd only just discovered, in a town full of bear shifters, with no job and no clear path forward. If Nico didn't want her to stay in Timber Ridge, there was no doubt that the town would support him, leaving her without any prospects.

Staying means being brave in ways I've never had to be before.

But looking down at Oakley's tear-stained face, feeling the trust and hope radiating from this little girl, Maddie realized something. She was falling in love. Not just with Nico, though the memory of his kiss still made her pulse race, but with Oakley too.

"I wish you could stay forever," Oakley whispered, pulling back to wipe her eyes. "Even if he won't admit it, Daddy's happier when you're around. I am too. We're better with you here."

Before Maddie could respond, heavy footsteps sounded on the porch. A knock echoed throughout the cabin, but she knew who it was.

"Come in."

The door opened, and Nico stepped in, but stopped quickly as he spotted them on the sofa together.

She realized the scene he saw. Oakley curled into Maddie's side, her arm over the young girl's shoulder. The empty hot chocolate mugs. It was a cozy scene.

Several emotions played out across Nico's face, making her want to go to him and smooth away the lines of worry and exhaustion.

"Oakley," he said gently. "I've been looking for you. You're supposed to tell me when you leave the house."

"I'm sorry, Daddy. I just needed..." Oakley glanced up at her. "I needed to talk to Miss Maddie."

"I see that." His gaze met hers, asking a silent question.

"She heard you on the phone and was upset," Maddie explained.

Nico's expression tightened with guilt. "Come on, sweetheart, let's get you home. It's almost time for dinner."

"I don't want to go yet." Oakley's arms tightened around Maddie. "Can't we stay a little bit longer?"

"Oakley—"

"Please, Daddy? Five more minutes?"

He looked at his daughter and then at Maddie, clearly torn. Finally, he sighed, shut the door, and moved into the cabin. But he didn't sit. He just stood there, arms crossed, watching them with a complicated expression that Maddie couldn't determine. He watched them as if he were trying to memorize the scene, like he knew it couldn't last.

"Your door should have been locked." The deepness in his voice was almost a growl.

Before she could respond, Oakley spoke.

"Uncle Grayson said Aunt Lucia might come for a visit for Christmas. Is that who you were talking to?"

"Yeah." He rubbed the back of his neck. "She's thinking about coming up for a few days. I told her we'd have to talk about it."

"Because of the rogue?" Oakley asked.

In that moment, Maddie realized shifter children grew up knowing about dangers human children never had to consider.

"Partly, but also because..." He glanced at Maddie. "Things are complicated right now."

"Why is everything always complicated? Why can't things just be easy for once?" Oakley muttered, echoing her earlier sentiment.

"I wish they could be, sweetie, I really do."

"If Miss Maddie stayed, would that make things easier? Then we'd be a real family and—"

"Oakley." Nico's voice was gentle but firm. "That's not how it works."

"Why not?" she demanded.

"Miss Maddie has her own life, her own plans. We can't just expect her to—"

"I don't have plans," Maddie interrupted, surprising herself. "That's kind of the problem. I have no job, apartment, or idea of what

I'm doing with my life. I came here to figure things out, but mostly I've just been..." She looked at Oakley, then at Nico. "I've been finding reasons to stay."

"Maddie..." Nico's expression was unreadable, but it called to her in ways she never knew possible.

"I'm not saying I'm staying. I'm saying...I don't want to leave. Not yet, maybe not at all." She let out a deep breath. "I realize it's complicated and there are a million reasons why it's a bad idea. But Oakley's right about one thing."

"What's that?" Nico asked.

"Sometimes adults make things more complicated than they need to be."

"Or sometimes things are actually complicated, and pretending they're not doesn't make them simpler."

"I'm not pretending. I'm saying maybe we don't have to figure everything out right now. Maybe we can just..." She gestured helplessly. "Take it one day at a time?"

"One day at a time," Oakley repeated, nodding enthusiastically. "That's perfect. So, you're staying?"

"At least for now," Maddie agreed, even though she wasn't entirely sure what she was committing to.

Oakley beamed and hugged her tightly. "Thank you!"

Over the girl's head, Maddie met Nico's gaze. He looked torn between hope and despair, like he wanted to believe what she said but wouldn't let himself.

"Come on, Oakley, we really need to get home."

Oakley reluctantly released Maddie and went to put on her coat. At the door, she turned back.

"Will you come up for dinner sometime? Daddy makes really good spaghetti. Then we could watch a movie afterward. Like a real family."

"Oakley—" Nico rubbed his temples.

"I'd love to," Maddie said. "Maybe this weekend?"

"Yes!" Oakley bounced with excitement as she bounded out the door, leaving Maddie and Nico standing in the doorway.

"You don't have to do that," Nico whispered.

"What if I want to?"

"Do you? Or are you just trying to make her happy?"

"Can't it be both?" She raised an eyebrow at him.

He looked at her, his amber eyes scanning her face. "You're really thinking about staying."

"Yes." That single word felt like she'd already made up her mind to call Timber Ridge home.

"Even though..." He glanced outside as if to make sure his daughter was out of earshot. "Even though you know what we are. What I am."

"Maybe especially because I know."

"That doesn't make sense." The lines across his forehead knitted together in confusion.

"Doesn't it?" She stepped closer. "For the first time in, well, I don't know how long, maybe my whole life, but I feel like I'm exactly where I'm supposed to be. Like, I'm not just going through the motions or doing what is expected. This feels real. Why wouldn't I want to stay?"

"Because real can hurt. Real is risky. Real means you could lose everything."

"Or I could gain everything." She touched his arm, feeling the heat of him even through his coat. "You told me your wife was your mate. That you knew she was the one. How did you know? How did you make that choice?"

"That's the thing, I didn't make the choice, it was inevitable. The moment I saw Elena, my bear knew. Just as I knew with you."

"Was it worth it? Even knowing how it ended, was loving her worth it?"

"Every second." There was no hesitation. "Every single second, even the painful ones. Elena was everything."

"Then you should understand my answer. Maybe risking pain is worth it if the alternative is never taking the chance at all."

He looked at her like she was breaking his heart while also healing it. "You don't know what you're saying."

"Maybe not completely, but I'm starting to figure it out." She squeezed his arm. "Go. Your daughter is waiting. But Nico? I'm not running away. So, you're going to have to stop running, too."

He opened his mouth and closed it, then just nodded. "Dinner. This weekend. Saturday?"

"It's a date."

"It's not a date. It's dinner with my daughter."

"Right. Not a date." She smiled. "Whatever you need to tell yourself."

A ghost of a smile touched his lips. "You're trouble, Maddie Garrett."

"You keep saying that like it's a bad thing." She smirked.

"It's a bad thing, but maybe it's also exactly what I need." He shook his head as he headed out the door. Striding up the path to where Oakley waited on the porch of the main house.

Maddie watched them go inside together, and the lights came on in the windows before Oakley's earlier words echoed through her thoughts. *We're better when you're here.*

Followed quickly by Nico's words: *Real means risks.*

Standing there in her rented cabin, watching the family that was starting to feel like hers, she smiled to herself. She had spent years playing it safe with Derek and with her job. Really, she had played it safe her whole life. Yet, where had it gotten her? Unemployed, heartbroken, and hiding in the mountains. It may be time to stop being safe and start being brave. Maybe it was time to choose the risk.

CHAPTER 12
CLOSE CALL

M addie woke to the sound of breaking branches. For a moment, she lay there frozen in bed, heart pounding. "It was just a dream."

But as the snap of wood came again, followed by heavy footsteps in the snow, and a low growl, she knew it was real.

She glanced at the bedside clock, 2:47 a.m.

Stay inside after dark. Nico's warning echoed in her head.

More sounds, closer now. Something was moving fast through the trees near the cabin. Not just something, but multiple people or animals. In the distance, she could hear voices too, but couldn't make them out, just the urgency in the tone.

Maddie pushed back the covers and crept out of bed. Staying in the shadows, she moved toward the window. The moon was bright enough to cast everything in silver light, and what she saw made her breath catch.

Nico stood in the clearing between the cabin and the tree line, wearing jeans and a heavy jacket, but despite the cold, no hat or gloves. Grayson was with him, along with three others, whom she recognized from the festival. They were spread out in loose formation, moving with predatory focus. Hunting.

"He went north," one of the men called, his voice carrying in the still air. "Toward the creek."

She pushed up the window just enough to allow her to hear them better, without causing too much of a draft.

"Stay behind him and the houses," Nico ordered, his voice sharp with authority. "Don't let him get past us."

"What if he shifts?" Grayson asked.

"Then we shift too. But try to keep this quiet. I don't want—" A crash from the tree line cut him off.

A figure burst from the woods. He was young, maybe early twenties. His clothes were torn, and his feet were bare despite the snow. Even from a distance, Maddie could see the wild look on his face. Desperate. His black hair matted, his face gaunt, and his eyes glowed amber in the moonlight.

"Please," the young man gasped, stumbling to a stop when he saw the men blocking his path. "Please, I'm not trying to cause trouble, I just need—"

"You're hunting on claimed territory." Nico's voice was stern. "You know the rules."

"I know, I'm sorry, I just...I don't have anywhere else to go. My clan—" The young man's voice broke. "They kicked me out. I've been alone for weeks, just trying to survive."

"By poaching deer and elk without permission? By leaving evidence everywhere?" Grayson moved closer, and Maddie saw his hands were tipped with claws. "You're going to get us all exposed."

"I swear I didn't know this area was claimed. I would have asked permission if I'd known."

"Bullshit," one of the other men growled. "You've been here for days. There's no way you didn't smell the markers."

The young shifter, cornered and afraid, backed up. "I'm sorry. I'll leave. I'll go and never come back."

"We can't just let you leave," Nico said, but there was compassion in his tone. "You're a mess. Barely in control of your animal. What clan were you with?"

"Centerville clan."

"Never heard of them." Nico glanced at Grayson and the others, who all shook their heads.

"We're small. Well, we were small. There was a challenge, and my alpha died. The new one didn't want—" The young man's voice cracked. "He didn't want weak ones. So, he cast us out."

Maddie listened to his words. *Cast out. Alone.* This wasn't a villain, rather, this was someone desperate and scared.

"What's your name?" Nico asked.

"Lee...Lee Foster."

"Okay, Lee. Here's what's going to happen. You're going to come with us. We'll get you fed and cleaned up. Then we're going to figure out what to do with you," Nico told him firmly. "But you need to understand, if you run, we will hunt you, and you won't like how that ends."

Lee's eyes went wide, and he glanced back toward the woods, as if he wanted to bolt. He was clearly still in fight-or-flight mode, but instead of running, he turned back to Nico. "How do I know you won't just kill me?"

"If I wanted you dead, you'd already be dead." Nico took a step forward, hands raised out in front of him. "I'm giving you a choice. Come peacefully, or we do this the hard way."

For a long moment, nobody moved. The tension in the air was thick enough to cut. Maddie wasn't out there, but still she held her breath waiting for Lee's answer.

Then Lee's shoulders sagged in defeat. "Okay."

"Smart choice." Grayson moved in to grab Lee's arm, but the young shifter flinched violently.

"Don't touch me!"

The reaction was pure instinct, but it set everything in motion.

Grayson lunged while Lee tried to run, and suddenly the clearing erupted into chaos.

Lee shifted mid-stride. One moment, a young man, and the next, a massive brown bear, smaller than Nico's bear but still terrifyingly large. He roared and swiped at Grayson, who partially shifted, claws extending as he dodged.

"Contain him!" Nico shouted. "Don't hurt him unless you have to."

The other men spread out, trying to circle Lee without getting too close. But the young bear was panicking, spinning and snarling, looking for an escape route.

His wild gaze locked on the cabin. More precisely, on Maddie's window.

"No!" Nico roared. He shifted faster than Maddie could track until his massive bear that dwarfed the others. He put himself directly between Lee and the cabin.

Lee hesitated, then made a break for the tree line on the opposite side of the clearing. Grayson and the others gave chase, their forms blurring between human and bear as they ran.

Nico held his position for a moment before he turned toward the cabin. Even in bear form, Maddie recognized his eyes, the distinctive amber-gold that haunted her dreams. He looked directly at her window, and she knew he could see her standing there. Then he turned and charged after the others, disappearing into the trees with a speed that shouldn't have been possible for something that large.

Maddie stood frozen at the window, her heart hammering so hard she felt dizzy.

She'd just watch men turn into bears. The complete transformation, right in front of her eyes. Not a partial shift or glowing eyes. Rather, the whole impossible, reality-breaking change. Intellectually, she'd known, Nico had told her, but now that she'd seen the evidence, it was undeniable. Knowing and seeing were two completely different things.

Her legs gave out, and she sank to the floor, her back against the wall, breathing hard.

"All of it is real," she mumbled to herself. Bear shifters existed, and Nico had transformed into a massive predator without hesitation.

She should be terrified. She should be packing her things and running back to the city and the world that made sense. But all she could think about was the protective stand Nico had taken. The way he'd positioned himself between the threat and the cabin. The warning in every line of his body as if to say: *You don't touch her. She's mine to protect.*

Her cell phone on the nightstand buzzed, making her jump.

With a deep breath, she reached for it. Nico's name glowed on the screen.

> Are you okay?

Her hands were shaking so badly that it took her three tries to respond.

> Yes. Are you?

> We've got him. He's contained. No one's hurt.

She let out a deep breath, thankful he was okay.

> What happens now?

> We talk to him. Figure out his story. Make a decision.

> Will you kill him?

The three dots appeared and disappeared several times.

> Not if we don't have to. He's young and scared, not malicious. We'll find a solution.

She stared at the message, her attention focusing on the fact that Nico wanted to find a solution. Not that Lee was a threat or that he was dangerous and needed to be eliminated. In her mind, a solution meant mercy if possible.

She thought of Lee's gaunt face, his desperate plea. The fact that he was cast out, alone, and struggling to survive.

Her phone vibrated in her hand with another text message from Nico.

> I'm sorry you had to see that.

> I'm not. I needed to see it. To really understand.

As she responded, she realized how true it was.

> And? Are you terrified?

She paused for a moment and really considered her answer. Was she terrified? Her heart was still racing, adrenaline still flooded her system, but underneath the fear was something else.

> A little afraid, but mostly I'm worried about you and about that kid.

> So, you're not running back to the city?

> No, I'm staying right here.

> Get some sleep. We'll talk in the morning.

Sleep was the last thing she wanted to do.

> Thank you for protecting me.

> Always.

That one word sent butterflies through Maddie's stomach. Knowing he had other things he needed to attend to, she forced herself to set the phone on the nightstand and climbed back into bed, though sleep wasn't going to come easily.

She could imagine Nico and the others dealing with Lee, making decisions about the frightened young shifter's fate.

She thought about chosen families and clan bonds. About the difference between power and cruelty. About the men who could turn into bears but chose mercy when they could have easily chosen violence. There was a world that was so much bigger and stranger than she'd ever imagined, and she had found herself in the center of it all. Instead of running, she was choosing to stay. She was no longer hiding. She was choosing this world and, more importantly, Nico. Even knowing what he was, perhaps especially knowing what he was, she was choosing this life.

The certainty of it settled over her like a warm blanket. Maddie had made her choice. She was staying. And nothing, not fear, logic, or even the voice in her head telling her that she was crazy, was going to change her mind.

CHAPTER 13
SISTER SECRETS

December twenty-third arrived as a cold, dreary day, with the sky heavy with the promise of snow. With coffee in hand, Maddie moved toward the window as noise attracted her attention. Even from this distance, she could hear a woman's voice, sharp and angry, along with Nico's deeper tones, equally furious.

"You can't just show up unannounced, Lucia!"

"It's my property too, Nico. I don't need your permission."

"You absolutely need to give me notice when there's—" His voice dropped too low for Maddie to hear.

"Don't give me that," Lucia snapped. "You're just pissed because I rented out the cabin without asking."

"You're damn right I'm pissed. You had no right—"

"I had every right!" Lucia cut him off again. "Stop acting like you're the only one who gets to make decisions."

Their voices rose and fell. The argument was clearly one that had been brewing for a long time. Maddie felt guilty for eavesdropping but couldn't quite make herself move away from the window.

A new car was parked in the driveway, a sleek silver sedan that looked painfully out of place among the trucks and SUVs typically seen in the Timber Ridge area. She assumed it was Lucia's.

A woman came into view. She was tall and slim, with her dark hair cut in a sharp bob. Her designer jeans and coat seemed ridiculously out of place.

Nico stepped around the house, his expression thunderous. "Running away. That's your answer to everything, isn't it, Lucia?"

"I'm not running away, I'm getting some air before I say something I'll regret." She whirled around to face him. "You know what your problem is? You think everyone should live by your rules, in your little kingdom, doing exactly what you want."

"That's not fair."

"Isn't it? You tried to control me my entire life. Where I went, who I saw, what I did with my future. And when I finally had enough and left, you acted like I'd betrayed the family."

"You did betray—" Nico cut himself off, dragging his hand through his hair. "You left without a word. You cut off contact with all of us for months. What was I supposed to think?"

"You were supposed to understand that not everyone wants this life." Her voice cracked slightly. "That maybe I needed something different. But you couldn't see past your own need to protect everyone."

"Someone has to protect you," Nico growled.

"From what? From living my own life?"

They stared at each other, and Maddie could almost see the resentment hanging in the air between them.

"Daddy?" A small voice from inside the house called out.

"Shit," Lucia muttered. "I didn't mean for Oakley to hear..."

But it was clearly too late. The screen door opened, and Oakley appeared in her pajamas, her face crumpling. "Why are you fighting?"

"We're not fighting, sweetie," Nico said, his voice immediately gentling. "We're just..."

"You're fighting. I heard you!" Tears spilled down Oakley's

cheeks. "I heard Aunt Lucia say she doesn't want to be here, and I heard you yelling."

"Oakley, sweetie, that's not—" Lucia started, but Oakley was already running.

Off the porch, across the snowy yard, and straight toward Maddie's cabin.

Maddie opened the door before Oakley could knock, and the little girl threw herself into her arms, sobbing.

"Hey, hey, it's okay." Maddie gathered her close, shooting a look at Nico and Lucia, who were both hurrying down the path. "Come inside, sweetie, you're freezing."

She ushered Oakley into the cabin and grabbed the blanket from the back of the sofa, wrapping it around the shivering girl. Through the window, she saw Nico and Lucia in a rapid and tense conversation before Nico jogged toward the cabin.

"I'm sorry," Oakley hiccupped. "I know I'm not supposed to come over without asking, but they were fighting so bad...I just..."

"Shhh, you don't need to apologize. You did the right thing." Maddie smoothed back Oakley's hair. "Do you want some hot chocolate?"

Oakley nodded, still crying.

As Maddie moved to the kitchen, Nico knocked once and entered. He looked around the cabin before his gaze centered on his daughter, curled up on the sofa in her pajamas and Maddie's blanket around her shoulders.

"Oakley—"

"I don't want to go back." Oakley stubbornly crossed her arms over her chest. "Not if you're going to keep fighting."

"We're not." Nico closed his eyes as if searching for patience. "Your aunt and I were just having a disagreement. That's all."

"It didn't sound like just a disagreement. It sounded like you hated each other."

"I don't hate your aunt. I could never..." He strolled around the sofa and crouched in front of her. "Sweetie, families fight sometimes. It doesn't mean we don't love each other."

"Then why is she leaving again? Why does everyone always leave?"

Maddie watched as Nico flinched, and guilt washed over his face.

"She's not leaving. She just got here and is going to stay through Christmas." He glanced at Maddie as if searching for help.

Before Maddie could respond, Lucia pushed open the front door and strolled in, looking significantly less polished than she had from a distance. Her eyes were red-rimmed, and her carefully applied makeup was smudged.

"Oak, I'm staying through Christmas."

Oakley looked between her father and aunt, clearly not convinced.

"How about this?" Maddie said, bringing over the hot chocolate. "Why don't you stay here with me for a bit? We could do some Christmas crafts. Maybe make decorations or cards. It will give your dad and aunt some time to talk things through properly."

"I don't want to be a bother—" Oakley whispered.

"You're never a bother." Maddie sat beside her on the sofa. "Besides, I could use the company and most definitely the creative help. I'm not very good at crafts, but I love doing them. Think you can help me?"

"Really?"

"Really. Once I tried to make a wreath, but it looked more like a big leafy blob."

That got a small smile from Oakley. "That's silly."

"I'm a silly person." Maddie looked at Nico. "If that's okay with you?"

He appeared to be torn between gratitude and something else, maybe reluctance to let his daughter stay with someone who might not stick around. But Oakley's hopeful expression seemed to decide for him.

"Okay, but just for a little while." He stood, his hand briefly touching Oakley's head. "Be good for Miss Maddie."

"I will."

As Nico moved to the door, Lucia still hovered awkwardly.

"Maddie?" She raised an eyebrow in question. "Sorry about the mix-up." Yet there didn't seem to be any remorse in her voice.

"It's fine," Maddie said evenly. "I'm Maddie Garrett. Thanks for taking Jackie's word on me and renting the cabin out."

"Lucia Matthews. I've known Jackie for years. If she said you were a good person who needed to get away, then I knew it was true." She looked around the cabin. "This place looks different. Better. Homey."

"Lucia," Nico said warningly.

"What? I'm giving her a compliment." But there was an edge to her voice. "Must be nice, playing house in someone else's space. Very cozy."

The tension in the room ratcheted up several notches.

"I'm paying rent," Maddie said, keeping her voice neutral despite the clear hostility. "I wasn't aware it was a problem."

"Oh, it's not a problem for me. I got my money." Lucia's smile was sharp. "Though I'm curious, what exactly are your plans here? This is supposed to be a vacation rental, not a permanent residence, and you seem to be getting awfully close to *my* family."

"Lucia," Nico said again, his voice harder.

"I'm just asking questions. She's living on *our* property, getting close to *our* family. I think I have a right to know what her intentions are."

"My intention is to mind my own business and not pick fights with people I just met," Maddie said, her patience wearing thin.

Lucia's eyebrows rose. "Did you just—"

"Okay, that's enough." Nico stepped between them, his tense muscles radiating his frustration. "Lucia, you and I need to finish our conversation. Maddie, thank you for watching Oakley. I'll come get her in an hour."

"Thank you, time," Maddie told him, her attention still on Lucia.

The other woman stared back, something almost like respect flickering in her expression before she masked it with indifference.

"Come on, Nico, let's go have that talk." Lucia turned and walked out the door and back toward the main house, her posture rigid.

Nico paused at the door. "I'm sorry about—"

"Don't apologize for her." Maddie softened slightly. "Go, we'll be fine here."

After Nico left and pulled the door shut behind him, Oakley let out a long breath. "Aunt Lucia doesn't like you."

"She doesn't know me."

"She doesn't like that Daddy likes you. She thinks you're going to hurt him."

Maddie looked at the perceptive little girl. "What do you think?"

"I think she's scared," Oakley said wisely. "She's scared that if she comes back, everything will be different. That she won't fit anymore. That's why she's taking it out on you, because you're new."

"That's very insightful." Maddie was surprised at how well Oakley understood what was happening around her and the emotions of grown-ups. She was unlike any other kid that Maddie had met before.

"I hear things." Oakley shrugged. "Shifter hearing, remember?"

"Right." Maddie looked around the cabin, trying to see what craft supplies she could come up with. "Okay, we could either make paper snowflakes or string popcorn for garland. Which one?"

"Both!" Oakley shouted.

Maddie gathered the supplies for the paper snowflakes and gave them to Oakley before heading to the kitchen to make popcorn. The moment Oakley settled down with a stack of paper and scissors, she began to relax, her natural cheerfulness returned. But Maddie couldn't stop thinking about Lucia's hostile assessment, and the accusations hidden within her questions.

What are your intentions here?

That was the question, wasn't it? What were her intentions? She wanted to stay, but was that possible? Would she be able to find employment in the small town? Would Nico give them a chance to see where things went between them? Or would he continue to push her away?

Through the window, she could see the main house and could imagine the difficult conversation happening inside. Siblings trying to bridge years of hurt and misunderstanding. A family trying to figure out how to be a family again.

Where did she fit in the picture? Was she welcome? Or just another complication in lives that were already complicated enough?

By the time Nico returned, Maddie and Oakley had paper snowflakes dangling on a string from the ceiling, and the popcorn garland was strung around the room. The entire room had a festive touch.

"Is everything okay?" Oakley asked him.

"We're getting there." He hugged her tightly.

Maddie noticed that his anger had been replaced with something softer, almost like resignation.

"Oakley, I'm sorry you had to hear all that."

"It's okay." She pulled back out of the hug to look at him. "Families fight. Miss Maddie said so."

"Miss Maddie is very wise." His gaze drifted to Maddie. "Thank you for everything."

"Anytime."

"Come on, Oakley." He grabbed her coat and held it out to her.

As they were leaving, Lucia appeared on the path, wrapped in a coat that was definitely not warm enough for the mountains. She looked younger without her defensive armor, more vulnerable.

"Oakley," she called softly. "I'm sorry about this morning. Can I get a hug?"

Oakley hesitated, then ran to her aunt. Lucia caught her and held tight. Maddie saw tears in her eyes.

"I love you," Lucia said into Oakley's hair. "I'm sorry I don't visit more. That's on me, not you. Okay?"

"Okay." Oakley pulled back. "Are you really staying for Christmas?"

"I am." Lucia smiled down at her.

"Good, because Miss Maddie is coming for dinner on Christmas Eve, it will be more fun if you're there too."

Both Lucia and Nico looked at Maddie in surprise.

"I...we talked about dinner. But I didn't know it was Christmas Eve," Maddie said, feeling suddenly awkward.

"Is that okay?" Oakley asked, looking between the adults. "Can Miss Maddie come for Christmas Eve dinner?"

Nico looked like he wanted to say several things, but instead just nodded. "If she wants to."

"I want to." Maddie nodded.

Lucia's expression was unreadable. "Well, this should be interesting."

As they walked back to the house, Lucia looked back at her, and when their gazes locked, Maddie saw a warning there. As if to say: *Don't hurt my family. Don't mess this up.*

Maddie held her gaze. *I'm not going anywhere.*

After a moment, Lucia's mouth quirked in something that might have been a smile. Then she turned and followed her brother and niece into the house.

Maddie closed the door and leaned back against it, her heart racing. Christmas Eve dinner with the whole family, including the hostile sister, who clearly thought Maddie was trouble. Then there was still the situation with the rogue shifter. This was going to be the most complicated Christmas of her life, yet somehow, despite everything, she was looking forward to it.

CHAPTER 14
THE BEAR KNOWS

Maddie was curled up in bed with a book in her hand when the soft knock came. She glanced at the clock, 10:47 p.m. Even in a place where nighttime patrols were normal, it was late for visitors.

Getting out of bed, she wrapped herself in her robe and padded toward the door. She glanced out the peephole and found Nico standing there, snowflakes melting in his dark hair. She opened the door and noticed the worn path in the fresh snow, as if he had been there for a while, pacing, trying to decide whether to knock.

"Hey," he whispered. "Is this too late?"

"No, come in."

He stepped inside, letting in cold air and the familiar scent of pine. He was still in the clothes from earlier, jeans and a thermal shirt that emphasized his broad shoulders, but he looked exhausted in a way that went beyond physical.

"I wanted to apologize for Lucia. For this morning and for all of it."

"You don't need to apologize for your sister." She closed the door and stepped further into the cabin.

"I do. She was hostile, and you didn't deserve that. She rented the cabin to you to get under my skin, but she had no right to come in here and be so rude." He ran his hand through his hair, a gesture of frustration she was starting to know well. "She's angry with me and took it out on you. That's not okay."

Maddie moved to the cabinet, where she stashed a bottle of whiskey she'd bought in town. "Want something to take the edge off?"

"Yes." He smiled tiredly.

She poured two glasses and handed him one as they settled on opposite ends of the sofa, a careful distance between them.

"How did the talk with Lucia go?" Maddie asked.

"About as well as you'd expect. We didn't solve anything." He took another sip. "She's staying through Christmas, which is more than I expected. Most importantly, she apologized to Oakley. That's what matters most to me."

"What is she so angry about?"

Nico stared into his glass as if looking for the words. "She felt suffocated growing up. The clan expectations, traditions, and the weight of our family legacy. I was the oldest, the heir apparent to lead the clan. She was just there. Expected to support, to follow, to accept her role." He looked up at Maddie. "I didn't realize how much pressure I was putting on her. How controlling I was being. I thought I was protecting her, but really, I was trying to keep everything from falling apart."

"After your parents died?"

"Yeah." He took a long sip from the glass before continuing. "They were killed in a car accident when I was twenty-two. Lucia was seventeen. Suddenly, I was responsible for her, the clan, and everything else. I'd just met Elena shortly before the accident, and she helped me through it. But Lucia...I failed her. I can see that now. I tried to be her parent, her alpha, and her brother all at once, and I did a shit job all around."

"You were grieving and trying to find your place in your new roles," Maddie reasoned.

"That's what Elena used to say. She'd tell me I was doing the best I could. She was always more understanding than I deserved."

Maddie took a sip of whiskey, feeling the burn, and she used it as encouragement. "Can I ask you something?"

"Anything."

"What was Elena like?"

Nico's expression flashed from grief to love to nostalgia. "She was light. That's the best way to describe her. Where I was intense or serious, she was joyful. She found happiness in small things and made everyone feel seen and valued. Oakley got her heart and generosity." He smiled sadly. "I knew it from the moment I met her that she was my mate."

"How does that work? The mate bond?"

He studied her for a moment as if deciding what to tell her. "It's different for every shifter. For me...I just looked at her, and my bear knew. Recognized her on some primal level as the other half. It's not logical or rational, it just is."

"And you knew immediately?"

"Within seconds of meeting her at a clan gathering. I was twenty, she was nineteen. One look and I knew." He finished his whiskey. "The human side usually takes longer to catch up with our animal."

"And when your mate dies?"

"It's like having a part of yourself ripped out. The bond doesn't break, it just...goes silent. Empty. If it weren't for Oakley, I wouldn't have survived the emptiness." He looked at her then, really looked at her. "I thought I'd never want anyone again. That I'd just go through the motions for Oakley's sake."

"But?" she pressed when he went silent.

"But then you showed up on my property, refusing to leave, driving me absolutely crazy." A small smile tugged at his mouth. "I started feeling things I thought I'd never feel again."

"Like what?" Her voice came out barely above a whisper.

He set down his glass and moved closer, closing the distance between them. "Like I want something for myself. Not just for Oakley, not for the clan, but for me."

"Tell me what you want."

He reached out and tucked a strand of hair behind her ear, his touch gentle despite the heat radiating from his skin. "You. I want you, Maddie, and that terrifies me."

"Why?"

"Because my bear..." He closed his eyes briefly, and when he opened them, they were glowing amber-gold. "My bear recognized you, too. Just like it recognized Elena. And I don't know what to do with that."

Maddie's breath caught in her throat. "You mean—"

"I mean, you're my mate. My second mate, which shouldn't even be possible. Most shifters only get one. But my bear is absolutely certain that you belong to us. That you're meant to be here." His hand cupped her cheek. "I've been fighting it because I didn't want to trap you, didn't want to force this on you, but I'm so tired of fighting, Maddie. I'm tired of denying what I feel."

"What do you feel?" she asked, her heart racing.

"Like I'm falling. You're the first real thing I've felt in years. Like if I kiss you right now, I might never stop."

"Then don't stop."

He made a sound low in his throat, part growl, part groan, and he kissed her.

It was different from their first kiss. Slower. Deeper. Not desperate and wild, but deliberate. Thorough. Like he was memorizing the taste of her, the feel of her, and the way she responded to his touch.

Maddie sank into it, and her hands reached up to grab hold of his shirt. He was warm, his body heat was almost feverish. When his tongue swept against hers, she gasped, and he took advantage, deepening the kiss until she was dizzy with it.

"Maddie," he murmured against her mouth. "Tell me to stop. Tell me this is a bad idea."

"It's a terrible idea," she agreed as she pulled him closer.

"We should slow down. Talk more. Make sure you understand what this means."

"Stop talking," she demanded.

He groaned and kissed her again, his hands sliding under her robe to find the tank top underneath. His palms were hot against her waist as he worked higher.

Maddie tugged at his shirt, and he pulled back just long enough to yank it over his head. In the low light, she could see the defined muscles of his chest and abdomen, the scattered scars that marked a life lived physically. His skin was flushed, radiating heat.

"You're burning up." She ran her hands over his chest.

"It's the bear. When we're aroused, our temperature rises. I'm trying to keep it under control, but with you..." He closed his eyes as her hands explored. "You make control very difficult."

"Good." She kissed his jaw, his throat, feeling his pulse hammering under her lips.

He made that growling sound again and lifted her, carrying her toward the bedroom with easy strength. She should have felt self-conscious. After all, she was only wearing a tank top and sleep shorts, no makeup, and her hair was in a messy topknot. But the way he looked at her, eyes glowing gold in the darkness, made her feel beautiful. Desired and even cherished.

In the bedroom, he laid her on the bed and followed her down, his weight a delicious pressure. They kissed again, hands roaming, exploring each other. When his mouth left hers to trail down her throat, Maddie arched into him, her fingers tangling in his hair.

"I've wanted this," he muttered against her skin. "Wanted you. Tried so hard not to."

"Why?"

"You deserve better than a widowed alpha with too much baggage and a six-year-old daughter."

She pulled him up to look at her. "Let me decide what I deserve."

Something cracked in his expression as the last of his resistance crumbled. He kissed her again, deeper, hungrier. His hands slid under her tank top, and she helped him pull it off. When his mouth found her breast, she gasped, her back arching.

His eyes were fully gold now, almost glowing in the darkness. When she looked down, she saw the tips of claws emerging from his fingertips where they gripped her.

"Nico," she breathed, part warning, part unsure of what she wanted.

"I know. I'm trying to control it." His voice was rougher, deeper. "But you make me want to shift if I'm not going to claim you. I want to mark you as mine in every way possible."

"Maybe I want that."

He groaned and kissed her again. She could feel the sharp points of fangs against her lip. The bear was so close to the surface, barely contained.

His phone rang. They both froze.

"Ignore it," Maddie whispered.

"I can't. Not at this hour." He pulled back, breathing hard, and grabbed his phone. "What?"

Maddie could hear Grayson's urgent voice on the other end.

"We've got a problem. Lee's gone. He broke out of the holding room and ran. We're tracking him now, but he's heading toward the residential area."

Nico's entire body went rigid. "How the hell did he get out?"

"No idea. But Nico, he's not in control. He's shifted, and he's panicking."

"I'm on my way." He hung up and looked at Maddie, regret written across his face. "I'm sorry. I have to—"

"I know. Go."

He leaned down and kissed her once more, deep and claiming. "We're not done here. Not even close."

"I'm holding you to that."

He snatched his shirt from the corner of the bed, pulled it on, and headed toward the living room to grab his coat. At the door, he paused. "Lock this behind me. Don't open it for anyone but me or Grayson. Understand?"

"Nico, I'll be fine."

"Maddie." His eyes flashed gold again. "Please, for me."

"Okay, I'll lock it," she assured him.

He nodded and was gone, the door closing behind him. Through the window, she saw him shift before racing toward the tree line where other shapes were already gathering.

Maddie locked the door and leaned against it. Her body was still humming with arousal, her lips swollen from his kiss.

Mate bond.

He'd said she was his mate. That his bear had recognized her, claimed her, wanted her with a certainty that transcended logic. All of that should freak her out and make her question her sanity for getting involved with someone who could literally turn into a bear, who came with a six-year-old daughter and a dead wife's memory and enough baggage to fill a cargo plane. But she felt certain.

This was right. He was right. Even if it was complicated, messy, and supernatural. It was better than anything else in her life.

She touched her lips, still feeling the ghost of his kiss and the press of fangs against her skin. Tonight, she learned what it felt like to be claimed by a bear shifter and discovered that she wanted nothing more than to claim him right back.

CHAPTER 15
UNWELCOMED GUEST

Maddie woke to a knock. Determined, insistent knocking that dragged her out of her dream of golden eyes and heated kisses. She glanced at the clock, 7:23 a.m. on Christmas Eve. The knocking came again.

"Coming," she called, grabbing her robe from the edge of the bed. She stumbled toward the door as she tried to tie it. Probably Oakley, excited about Christmas Eve dinner, or maybe Nico, coming to finish what they started before the emergency.

She opened the door and froze.

Derek stood on her porch, holding a carrier with two cups of coffee and a white bakery bag. He looked exhausted. Dark circles under his eyes, his usually neat hair disheveled, and his clothes rumpled from the long drive. But there he stood, smiling that boyish, apologetic smile that used to be her weakness, making her forgive him for anything.

"Surprise," he announced. "I know I should have called, but I was afraid you'd tell me not to come."

For a moment, Maddie stood there, her brain struggling to process. Derek was there on her porch in Timber Ridge.

"I told you not to come," she snapped. "What are you even doing here?"

"I couldn't spend Christmas without you." He held up the coffee carrier. "I brought your favorite. That stupid caramel macchiato thing you love and croissants. Can I come in? It's freezing out here."

She wanted to tell him no. To tell him to leave. Showing up like this wasn't okay. But shock and years of habit made her step back, which he took as an invitation.

Derek entered the cabin, dropped his overnight bag by the door, and looked around with barely concealed disdain. "Wow. This is... cozy. Really rustic."

"What are you doing here, Derek?" Maddie asked again.

"I came to see you. To talk to you." He set the coffee and bakery bag down on the counter. "I wanted to apologize properly, face to face, the way I should have weeks ago."

"I told you we're done."

"I know you said that, but Maddie, come on. We've been together for years. That must mean something. You can't just throw that away without giving me a chance to make things right."

"*You* broke up with me right after I lost my job. *You* said we wanted different things. Remember?"

"I was an idiot." He took a step closer to her, his expression earnest. "I was scared about the future, about money, and all these adult responsibilities I've been avoiding. Instead of talking to you about it, I panicked and ended things. But I've had time to think and realize now that I've made a huge mistake."

Acutely aware of her tank top and shorts, she pulled the robe tighter around her. "Derek—"

"Just hear me out, Maddie, please." He pulled out a barstool and sat. "Come, have your coffee, and let me say what I came all this way to say."

Against her better judgment, she sat. Derek handed her a coffee, and the first sip was a familiar taste that was comforting and wrong, like putting on an old sweatshirt that no longer fit quite right.

"I've been miserable without you," Derek said, sitting across from her. "The apartment feels empty, and everything reminds me of you. The more time passes, the more I realize I don't want a life without you in it."

"You seemed pretty sure a month ago."

"I was being stupid. Reactionary. I let the stress get to me instead of leaning on you, on us." He reached across the table, taking her hand. "But I'm here now. I'm willing to do the work. Couples therapy, whatever you want. We can figure this out."

Maddie looked down at their joined hands, and she felt nothing. It was pleasant enough, but not electric. Not the way Nico's touch made her skin tingle, made her heart race.

"What about the things you said?" she asked quietly. "About wanting different things? About me being too focused on my career? Or you not being ready to settle down?"

"I was lashing out. I said things I didn't mean because I was scared." He squeezed her hand. "The truth is, I love you. I want to build a life with you. Marriage, kids, the whole thing. Isn't that what you want?"

It was what she'd wanted. Three months ago, she would have said yes without hesitation. But now...

"I don't know what I want anymore," she said honestly.

"Come home with me, and we'll figure it out." His voice turned coaxing. "Whatever's going on up here, whatever you think you're finding...it's not real, Maddie. It's a fantasy. A break from reality. But you can't hide in the mountains forever."

"I'm not hiding."

"Aren't you? You came up here to lick your wounds after I hurt you. I get that. But now it's time to come back. To deal with real life. Real problems and relationships."

Movement outside the window caught Maddie's attention. Nico had emerged from the main house, and from the way his body turned toward the unfamiliar silver sedan parked near Maddie's cabin, she knew he'd spotted the visitor. His body language was rigid and tense. Protective and possessive in equal measure.

Their eyes met across the snowy yard, and even though she couldn't see the color from here, she knew they'd be glowing gold.

"Who's that?" Derek questioned.

"My landlord."

"He looks pissed. Did you not pay rent or something?"

"He's just protective of his property." The words felt like a betrayal, reducing Nico to something so much less than what he was.

"Weird." Derek turned back to her, reclaiming her attention. "So, what do you say? Can we talk about this? Really talk, not just text messages and phone calls?"

"You drove all this way. I guess we should talk."

His face lit up. "Thank you. That's all I'm asking for...a chance." He glanced around the cabin again. "This place is pretty small. Is there somewhere we could go? Get breakfast, maybe?"

The thought of taking Derek into town, parading him in front of the shifter community that had just started to accept her, made Maddie's stomach turn.

"There's only one diner, and it's probably packed on Christmas Eve."

"Then we can stay here, eat these croissants, and catch up." He smiled that familiar smile. "Tell me what you've been doing up here. Besides, apparently making your landlord territorial."

Before Maddie could respond, heavy footsteps sounded on the porch, followed by a single sharp knock.

Derek looked annoyed. "Does he always just show up?"

Maddie ignored him and headed toward the door. When she opened it, she found Nico standing there, his expression carefully controlled but his eyes blazing gold. He'd thrown on a coat but hadn't bothered to button it, and she could see the rapid rise and fall of his chest.

"Maddie." His voice was level, but she heard the edge underneath. "Is everything okay?"

"Everything's fine. This is—"

"Derek." Derek appeared behind her, extending his hand with professional politeness. "Derek O'Hair, Maddie's boyfriend."

"Ex-boyfriend," Maddie corrected quickly.

Nico's gaze flicked to Derek's outstretched hand, but he didn't take it. "Nico Matthews. I own this property."

An awkward beat of silence.

Derek lowered his hand. "Right. The landlord. Nice to meet you."

"What are you doing here?" Nico questioned without his gaze wavering from her.

"Visiting Maddie for Christmas. We have a lot to talk about." Derek's arm wrapped around Maddie's shoulders, casual yet possessive. "I'm trying to convince her to come home where she belongs."

Nico's jaw tightened, and Maddie saw the tips of his claws emerge from his fingertips before he forced them back.

"Maddie can make her own decisions about where she belongs," Nico said, his voice dangerously soft.

"Of course she can. I'm just reminding her what she's missing back in the city." Derek's grip tightened slightly. "Real life, opportunities, and relationships."

"Derek," Maddie warned and shrugged out of his embrace.

But the damage was done. Nico's eyes were fully gold now, his control visibly fraying. "Maddie, can I talk to you? Privately?"

"We're in the middle of something," Derek said before Maddie could respond.

"I wasn't talking to you." Nico's voice dropped lower, that alpha authority creeping in. "Maddie, please."

"Give us a minute," Maddie said to Derek.

"Maddie—"

"Just a minute."

She stepped outside, closing the door behind her. The cold air hit her face, but Nico's body heat radiated like a furnace, even standing a few feet away.

"Are you okay?" he asked immediately.

"I'm fine. Surprised, but fine."

"Did you know he was coming?"

"Before I blocked his number, he texted me to tell me he was coming. I told him no. I didn't even think he knew where I was going. Unless the friend who connected me with Lucia told him where the cabin was." She shook her head.

"Do you want him here?"

That was the question, wasn't it? Did she want Derek here, trying to resurrect something that had been dying long before he'd officially ended it?

"No," she admitted honestly. "But he drove all this way. I should at least hear him out."

"Should you?" Nico took a step closer, and she could see the gold bleeding through his irises, the bear right there beneath his skin. "Or are you just being polite because you're uncomfortable saying what you really want?"

"What do you think I really want?"

"I think you want to tell him to leave. To go back to his real life and his real opportunities and let you figure out your own path." His voice was rough. "I think you want him gone so we can finish what we started last night."

Heat flooded through her at the memory of his mouth on hers and his hands on her skin.

"Maybe I do," she admitted. "But I can't just kick him out. That's not who I am."

"Even though he kicked you out when it was convenient for him?"

"That's different," she bit out in annoyance.

"Is it?"

Through the window, she could see Derek pacing the small

cabin, looking at his phone, clearly impatient, just as he always was when he had to wait on anything.

"He's expecting me to come back. Expecting that I'll have gotten this out of my system and be ready to return to *normal*," Maddie said quietly.

"Will you?"

She looked up at Nico, the man who had told her the night before that his bear recognized her as his mate, and realized nothing about this was normal. Nothing about this was safe or logical or the kind of choice her old self would have made. But then again, her old self had been miserable.

"No." She shook her head. "I'm not going back."

He let out a soft breath as relief washed over his face. "You're sure?"

"I'm sure. I just need to make him understand that."

"Do you want me to—"

"No, I need to do this myself." She touched his arm, felt the barely controlled power thrumming beneath his skin. "But thank you for checking on me."

"Always." He covered her hand with his, the contact sending sparks through her. "Maddie, about last night—"

"Tonight," she said. "We'll talk tonight after Derek leaves and after Christmas Eve dinner. Once everything settles."

"You're still coming to dinner?"

"Try to stop me." She smirked.

A smile tugged at his mouth. "I wouldn't dream of it."

He turned and stepped off the porch, leaving her to handle Derek. But as she watched him walk back to the main house, she could feel the weight of everything unsaid and everything building between them. She'd already made her decision about staying. Now, as she opened the door to the cabin, she realized she needed to get rid of Derek quickly to enjoy the evening.

Derek looked up from his phone as she entered. "What was that about?"

"He was checking to make sure everything was okay."

"Seems a little overprotective for a landlord."

"It's a small community. Here, people look out for each other."

Derek studied her face. "Maddie, is there something going on between you and that guy?"

"We're friends."

"Friends." It wasn't a question, but it was clear in his voice that he wasn't convinced. "The way he looked at me...that wasn't friendly, Maddie. That was possessive."

"Derek—"

"I'm not trying to start a fight. I'm just trying to understand what's happening here." He slipped his phone back into his pocket and moved closer. "You're different. This place is changing you."

"Maybe it is, and maybe I need to change."

"Into what? A mountain hermit who hides from her problems?"

"I'm not hiding," she defended. "I'm finally figuring out what I actually want instead of just accepting what other people think I should want."

"What do you want?" Derek asked.

Before she could answer, her phone buzzed. She pulled it out of her robe pocket and saw a text from Oakley, sent from Nico's phone.

> Daddy said you're still coming. You are right? I'm so excited!

Maddie smiled despite the tension.

> Still coming. Wouldn't miss it.

"What's that?" Derek asked, the annoyance clear in his voice.

"Dinner plans. Tonight's Christmas Eve after all." She pocketed the phone and looked back at Derek.

"With the possessive landlord?"

"With his daughter and his sister. It's a family thing."

"A family thing." Derek's expression hardened. "Maddie, what the hell is going on here? You're having family dinners with strangers while your actual family, heck, your actual life, is waiting for you at home?"

"That's not *my* home anymore, Derek. Don't you get that? Being with you, doing the same thing, living the same life I was living...it wasn't making me happy."

"And hiding in the mountains makes you happy?"

"Yes." She nodded. "It actually does."

They stare at each other. The years of history hung between them. That's when Maddie realized with absolute clarity that it was over. Not because of Nico, though he was part of it, but because Derek represented everything she'd been running from. The safe choice, the expected path, the life that looked good on paper but felt empty in reality.

She wanted more than that. She wanted magic, and she wanted risk. She wanted a man who looked at her as if she were both his salvation and his doom. She wanted a little girl who made her heart ache with hope and possibility. Most of all, she wanted a life that felt real, even if it was impossible.

"Derek," she said gently. "I'm sorry you drove all this way, but I'm not coming back."

"Don't say that." The corner of his mouth turned downwards, clearly disappointed. "Don't decide right now when you're emotional, and I just showed up—"

"I'm not being emotional, I'm being honest. Derek, we're done. If I'm being honest, we've been done for a long time. We just didn't want to admit it."

"Maddie—"

"You deserve someone who's all in. Someone who wants the same things you want, and who doesn't need to run to the mountains to figure out her life." She took his hand, squeezing it once. "I deserve to figure out who I am without you, without anyone telling me who I should be."

He looked like he wanted to argue and try to convince her she was making a mistake. But maybe he saw something in her expression, the determination or just the simple truth that she meant every word.

"Is it him?" he asked quietly.

"It's not about him, it's about me. About finally choosing what I want instead of what's safe."

"And what you want is here? In this tiny town in the middle of nowhere?" The surprise was thick in his voice.

She looked out the window toward the main house on the hill, where smoke curled from the chimney, and Christmas lights twinkled in the morning sun. "Yeah, I think it is."

CHAPTER 16
COMING HOME

Dressed in jeans and a sweater, Maddie stood on the porch as Derek tossed his overnight bag back into the car. His jaw clenched, frustration and hurt flickered across his face. He'd assumed she'd take him back. The assumption left her torn between guilt and relief.

"This is a mistake," he said through the open car door. "You're going to realize that when reality sets in. When the fantasy wears off, and you're stuck here with no job and no future."

"Derek, I'm sorry, I really am, but this is what I need."

He looked at her, and she saw the moment he knew she really meant it. With a brief nod, he started the engine. "I hope you know what you're doing."

"I don't, but I'm doing it anyway," she said, knowing full well he couldn't hear her as he'd already slammed his door.

The silver sedan disappeared down the mountain road, and the weight of his presence that had been around her neck since she'd opened the door disappeared.

Maddie stood on the porch for another minute, letting the reality of her choice settle over her. For a second, she wondered if she'd regret it. They'd been together for years, and it had been comfortable until the end. Now she was letting go of the safe and choosing the unknown.

She looked up at the main house, where she could see Nico in the window, watching. She had no doubt that he'd seen Derek leave.

Without hesitation, she strolled up the path. At the main house, she knocked once, and Nico opened the door almost immediately. She'd seen him earlier but hadn't realized how exhausted he looked. The dark circles under his eyes warned her he hadn't slept much, no doubt dealing with the rogue situation. While the tension in every line of his body had everything to do with the situation that he'd witnessed with Derek.

"Is he gone?" Nico asked.

"He's gone."

"Are you okay?"

"I'm terrified," Maddie admitted. "This is crazy. Everything about this is crazy, but I'm staying."

Something shifted in his expression, hope warring with caution. "You're sure."

"No, but I'm choosing it anyway." She stepped inside, and he closed the door behind her. "But before we talk about us, I need to know what happened last night. Did you find Lee?"

Nico's expression softened. "We found him. It took a few hours, but we tracked him down near the creek. He'd shifted back to human form and was just sitting there in the snow, sobbing."

"Is he okay?"

"He's scared. Traumatized. His alpha didn't just kick him out, he threatened to kill him if he ever came back. Told him that he was weak and the clan didn't need dead weight." His voice was tight with anger. "He's barely twenty-two, Maddie. Just a kid who's been on his own for months, surviving."

"What's going to happen to him?"

"We talked for hours. I was coming home when I saw Derek's car and came to the cabin. It's been a long night. But Grayson and a few other senior clan members and I voted." His gaze met hers. "We're taking him in. Officially. He'll join our clan."

"Really?" Relief flooded through her.

He nodded. "Lee needs guidance, training, and a stable clan structure. We have room for him. Grayson is setting him up in the old hunting cabin on the north side of the property. He'll work for me doing property maintenance and helping with the Christmas tree farm operations. He'll have to learn to control his shifting, understand clan dynamics, and become part of the community, but with time, he can do it. He'll be a good addition to our clan."

"That's really generous of you."

"It's the right thing to do. Everyone deserves a second chance, and everyone deserves a family." He smiled slightly. "Besides, Oakley already adopted him. She brought him cookies this morning and informed him he's now her big brother. He cried. He's never had a true family, and she made him feel accepted."

With tears in her eyes, she reached out and took his hand. "You're a good man, Nico Matthews."

"I'm trying to be." He stepped closer. "Having you here makes me want to be better. Makes everything better."

She stepped closer and reached up to touch his face. "Good, because I'm choosing you. I'm choosing Oakley. I'm choosing this impossible, supernatural, complicated situation over the safe life I had before, because safe wasn't making me happy."

"Maddie—"

"I know it's fast, and it's probably insane. There are likely a million reasons why this shouldn't work, but I don't care." She reached up and touched his face. "I'm all in, Nico. That is, if you'll have me."

He growled low in his throat as he pulled her inside, closing the door behind them.

"If I'll have you?" His hands framed her face. "I've been yours since the moment you opened that door and refused to leave. My bear knew. I was just too stubborn to admit it."

"And now?"

"Now I'm done being stubborn." He kissed her, deep and claiming. "You're my mate, Maddie. My second chance, and I'm not letting you go."

This kiss was different from all the others. It wasn't desperate, interrupted, or tinged with uncertainty. It was a promise. A claim and a beginning.

When they finally pulled apart, both breathing hard, Nico pressed his forehead to hers.

"I love you," he said quietly. "I know it's too soon to say it, but I do. I love you."

Maddie's heart felt like it might burst. "I love you too. I think I have for a while now."

They kissed again, slower this time, savoring. For the first time, there were no interruptions, emergencies from rogue shifters, or family drama. It was just the two of them, finally on the same page.

"Where's Oakley?" Maddie asked when they came up for air.

"With Emma. They're making cookies for tonight." He smiled. "She's been talking about Christmas Eve dinner nonstop and about you being there."

"Speaking of which, I should probably go get ready. What time should I come up?"

"Six, but Maddie?" He caught her hand. "After tonight, after Christmas, we need to talk. About the mate bond, about what it means and how this works."

"I know, and I want to know all of it, every detail." She squeezed his hand. "But tonight, let's just be. No heavy conversations. Just family, Christmas, and being happy."

"I can do that."

She started to leave, but he pulled her back for one more kiss. "Thank you," he murmured against her lips. "For staying. For choosing us and for caring about what happens to Lee."

"Of course I care. He's part of your clan now. Which means he's part of my family too."

The look Nico gave her was so full of love and pride that it took her breath away.

"You're going to fit in perfectly here," he said.

"I hope so."

"I know so."

The rest of the day passed in a blur of preparation. Maddie showered and changed into her favorite forest green sweater and her nicest jeans. She'd packed light when she'd come to Timber Ridge, never expecting to need anything fancy. Yet, this felt right. Casual and comfortable, like being welcomed into someone's home.

At 5:45 p.m., she grabbed the bottle of wine she had picked up in town but never opened and walked up to the main house. Through the windows, she could see people moving around, and laughter and music drifted toward her.

She knocked, and Oakley flung open the door, practically vibrating with excitement.

"You came! You look so pretty." Oakley grabbed her hand and pulled her inside. "Come see the tree and the cookies. Wait until you meet everyone. This Christmas is going to be the best."

The main house was warm and welcoming, decorated with an eclectic mix of handmade ornaments and evergreen garlands. A massive Christmas tree dominated the living room, covered in lights and decorations that looked like they'd been collected over generations. The scents of pine, cooking, and cinnamon filled the air.

There were more people gathered than Maddie had expected. Grayson was there with a woman who must be his wife. Kate Watson from the general store was laughing with an older man. Sarah and her husband, the couple with the baby Maddie, had met at the festival.

There were at least a dozen others, all taught and laughing, creating a warm atmosphere of family chaos. They all turned when Maddie entered, and for a moment, she felt as if she were being assessed again.

Then Kate broke the silence. "Well, it's about time! We've been waiting to officially meet Nico's mate."

Warmth flooded through Maddie as the group welcomed her with smiles and greetings. Not as a stranger or an outsider, but as someone who belonged.

Nico appeared from the kitchen, wiping his hands on a towel, and his entire face transformed when he saw her. He crossed the room and kissed her cheek, a casual gesture of affection that somehow felt momentous in front of his extended family.

"Everything, this is Maddie, my mate," he announced.

The words sent a thrill through her. His mate. Not his girlfriend, not his date, but his mate.

"Finally!" Sarah hollered, grinning. "We've been telling him for weeks that he needs to stop being stubborn and just claim you already."

"Sarah," Nico said warningly, but with a smile on his face.

"What? It's true. The whole clan could smell it on both of you. The mate bond doesn't lie."

Lucia appeared from upstairs, and Maddie tensed slightly. But the other woman's expression was softer than it had been the last time they were face-to-face.

"Maddie," she said, moving down the stairs. "Can we talk? Just for a minute?"

Nico looked like he wanted to protest, but Maddie nodded. "Of course."

They stepped into the kitchen, away from the noise of the living room. Lucia leaned against the counter, studying Maddie with sharp, assessing eyes.

"I owe you an apology for being hostile. You didn't deserve that."

"You were protecting your family, and I understand that."

"Maybe, but I was also being petty and jealous." Lucia smiled ruefully. "I left because I didn't want this life, this responsibility. Then you show up, and within a few weeks, you're everything I couldn't be—accepted by the clan, loved by my niece, making my brother happy for the first time in years. It made me feel... replaceable."

"You're not replaceable. You're Oakley's aunt and Nico's sister. That's not something anyone else can be."

"I know, and rationally, I'm happy for him and for all of you. Nico deserves this. He deserves someone who wants to be here, who chooses this life." She met Maddie's gaze. "But I need to know, are you sure? Because if you're going to leave, if you're going to break his and Oakley's hearts, do it now. Before they get even more attached."

"I'm not leaving."

"Even though it means giving up your old life? Your career, your plans, and everything you thought you wanted?"

"Especially because of that." Maddie moved closer. "I spent years in a relationship that was slowly suffocating me, working a job that made me miserable, living a life that looked good on paper but felt empty. This—" She gestured toward the living room where laughter and warmth spilled out. "This feels real. Your brother feels real. Same with Oakley. I'm not giving this up."

Lucia studied her for a second and then nodded. "Okay. Then welcome to the family. Fair warning, we're loud, nosy, and we will absolutely meddle in your life."

"I can handle it."

"Good." Lucia held out her hand. "Truce?"

Maddie took it and shook it. "Truce."

They returned to the living room, where Nico immediately came to Maddie's side, his hand settling on the small of her back.

"Everything okay?" he murmured as he leaned down to her ear.

"Everything's perfect."

Dinner was chaotic and wonderful. The long table could barely hold everyone, with multiple conversations happening at once, food being passed around family-style, Oakley chattering nonstop about everything from her Christmas wish list to the snowman she and her cousin had built earlier.

Maddie sat between Nico and Oakley, feeling accepted in a way she'd never experienced. These people had accepted her as one of their own.

After dinner, as people were having dessert and coffee, Grayson stood up and tapped his glass.

"I want to propose a toast," he said. "To Lee, who we've officially welcomed into our clan as of this afternoon."

Sarah glanced toward Nico in surprise, and he added. "We talked to him and got his full story. He was telling the truth. His clan fell apart, and he's been on his own for months. He's young, scared, and needs guidance. So, we're giving him a chance."

"He's staying?" Sarah questioned.

"He's staying. We set him up in the old hunting cabin on the north side of the property. He'll work for me and be part of our community as he learns to control his shifting better."

"Everyone," Grayson continued, his gaze drifting toward Maddie. "Deserves a family, a clan, and a place to belong. So tonight, we welcome two new members, Lee, who we'll introduce properly soon, and Maddie, who's already stolen our alpha's heart and made his daughter happier than we've seen her in years."

"To Lee and Maddie!" the group chorused, raising their glasses.

Maddie felt tears prick her eyes as she raised her own glass. This was what family felt like. Not perfect, not simple, but real, warm, and accepting.

After dinner, as people were bundling up to leave, Kate pulled Maddie aside.

"I knew," she said with a knowing smile. "The moment you walked into my store. I told Thomas that you were Nico's mate. He didn't believe me, but a grandmother knows these things."

"You could tell just by looking at me?"

"I could tell by the way you asked about him. The way your eyes light up when you talked about Oakley, and by the way Nico looked at you at the festival, like you were the answer to every prayer he didn't know he's been praying." Kate patted her hand. "Welcome home, dear. We're glad you're here."

After everyone left, it was just Nico, Maddie, Oakley, and Lucia. They sat in the living room, the Christmas tree lights casting a warm glow, while Oakley tried valiantly to stay awake.

"Can we open one present?" Oakley asked, yawning. "Please!"

"One," Nico agreed. "But then bed. Santa can't come if you're still awake."

Oakley chose a small package wrapped in silver-and-blue paper. She opened it carefully, revealing a delicate silver bracelet with a small bear charm.

"It's from all of us," Lucia said. "To remind you that you're never alone. That you always have your family and clan."

Oakley's eyes filled with tears. "It's perfect." She looked at Maddie. "Do you have a present?"

"Oakley," Nico said gently. "Maddie is our guest. She doesn't need to—"

"Actually," Maddie said, pulling a small wrapped box from her pocket, "I have something for you."

Oakley tore into the wrapping.

"That's two." Nico chuckled at his daughter.

"Daddy..." But she didn't stop, she continued to lift the lid of the box and revealed a simple leather cord with a small crystal pendant. "It's beautiful! What kind of crystal is it?"

"Rose quartz. It's supposed to represent love and family. I found it in town and thought of you."

Oakley threw her arms around Maddie's neck. "Thank you. I love it. I love you!"

The words were said with such sincerity that Maddie felt her chest tighten. "I love you too, sweetie."

"Alright, Oakley, it's time for bed." Nico stood and reached down to lift a yawning Oakley into his arms and carry her to bed. "I'll be right back."

"Take your time." She leaned back against the sofa, her gaze following him as he headed up the steps with Oakley snuggling against him.

"Goodnight, Miss Maddie." Oakley's voice was soft as they disappeared.

As Nico put Oakley to bed, Maddie rose from the sofa and headed to the kitchen to clean up after the family dinner. She cleaned off the plates and stacked them in the dishwasher before turning toward the pots and pans. While Lucia dealt with the leftovers.

"Leave it," he said. "We'll deal with it tomorrow."

"You sure?" Lucia asked as she placed a bowl in the dishwasher. "I'm pretty sure there are eighteen pots and pans, and I can—"

"I'm sure. Go to bed. You're in the guest room, remember?"

Lucia looked between them, a knowing smile on her face. "Right. I'll be in the guest room with earplugs in."

"Lucia!" Nico looked at his sister.

She laughed and headed upstairs, calling back, "Merry Christmas to all, and to all a good night!"

Alone, Nico pulled Maddie into his arms. "So, how was your first clan Christmas Eve?"

"Perfect. Overwhelming yet wonderful." She rested her head against his chest, listening to his steady heartbeat. "I can't believe this is my life now."

"Is it?"

"I mean..." She pulled back to look at him. "I need to find a job, figure out living arrangements, and all that practical stuff, but yes. This is my life now. If you'll have me."

"If I'll have you," he repeated, smiling. "Maddie, I want you to stay. In the cabin, in town, in my life. In Oakley's life. I want you here permanently as my mate."

"Even though it's fast?"

"Shifters don't do slow. When we know, we know, and Maddie, I know." He cupped her face. "I love you. My bear loves you. Oakley loves you. The clan has accepted you. All that's left is for you to say yes."

"Yes." She smiled up at him. "Yes, to all of it."

He kissed her, deep and thoroughly, and when they pulled apart, his eyes were glowing gold.

"Stay tonight," he whispered. "Stay every night. Make this house a home again."

"What about Oakley? Lucia?"

"Oakley has been not-so-subtly asking when you're going to move in. And Lucia leaves tomorrow night. Then it will just be us. Our family. What do you say?"

She thought about the cabin, her temporary refuge that had become so much more. About the life she'd left behind and about Derek driving away, allowing that last door to her old self to close. She thought about Nico's gold eyes and Oakley's bright smile. The clan of bear shifters who'd welcomed her like she belonged.

"I say yes," her voice low. "To all of it. To you, this, and to us."

He kissed her again, and this time, when he lifted her and carried her toward the stairs, there were no interruptions. Just the two of them, finally together, finally home.

Merry Christmas, indeed.

CHAPTER 17
CLAIMED

Maddie wrapped her arms around Nico's neck, her heart racing with anticipation, as he carried her up the stairs. Tonight, she'd finally claim her bear. There wouldn't be any further interruptions.

Outside of Oakley's room, he paused, and they listened for a moment. Soft, even breathing came from within. The young girl was deeply asleep, exhausted from the excitement of Christmas Eve.

"She's out," he whispered. "She'll sleep through the night."

"Good." She looked up at him. "That means you're mine tonight."

Without comment, he continued down the hall, past the guest room where Lucia was presumably already asleep, to the end where his bedroom door stood open.

Inside, the room was unmistakably his. Masculine and simple, with heavy wooden furniture and deep green bedding. A window overlooked the forest, moonlight streaming through to paint everything in a silver light. Photos on the dresser caught her attention. Oakley as a baby, a wedding photo of him and Elena, the two of them looking impossibly young and happy.

Nico saw where she was looking as he set her down gently. "I can put those away—"

"No. She was your wife, Oakley's mother. She should be here." Maddie turned to face him. "I'm not trying to replace her. I couldn't even if I wanted to."

"You're not replacing her. You're..." His words trailed off as if he was struggling for the right ones. "You're different. What I feel for you is different. Elena was my first love, my first mate. But you, Maddie, you're my second chance. My future."

He pulled her close, his hands settling on her waist. Even through her clothes, she could feel the heat of him.

"Are you sure about this?" he asked, his voice rough. "About us? Because once we do this, once the bond is sealed, there's no going back. You'll be mine, and I'll be yours, forever."

"I've never been more sure of anything in my life." She reached up and touched his face, feeling the barely controlled power thrumming beneath his skin. "Make me yours, Nico."

He kissed her, and it was like a dam breaking. All the tension and all the waiting came crashing together. He slid his hands into her hair before gliding them along her back and pulling her impossibly closer.

She grabbed his shirt and pulled it over his head, breaking the kiss just long enough to get rid of the fabric. Then her hands were on his bare chest, feeling the heat of his skin, the rapid beat of his heart.

His hands found the hem of her sweater. "Can I?"

"Please."

He pulled it off slowly, reverently, his gaze tracking every inch of exposed skin. Then her bra joined in on the floor, and he looked at her, his eyes blazing gold.

"Beautiful, so beautiful."

He backed her toward the bed, his mouth finding hers again as they fell together onto the soft mattress. His weight pressed her down, solid, warm, and right.

They took their time exploring. Hands and mouth discovering sensitive places, learning what made the other gasp or moan. He was gentle despite his obvious strength, his touches reverent even as his control visibly frayed.

When the rest of their clothes were gone, and nothing separated them, he paused, looked down at her with those glowing eyes.

"I love you," he said. "I need you to know that. This isn't just the mating bond or physical need. I love you, Maddie."

"I love you too." She pulled him down for a kiss. "Now stop being noble and make love to me."

He smiled against her mouth. "Demanding."

"You like it."

"I love it, just as I love you."

When they finally joined, it was overwhelming in the best way. Maddie gasped at the sensation and the heat of him. The feeling of completeness was something she'd never experienced before.

Nico held himself still, letting her adjust, his whole body trembling with restraint. "Okay?"

"More than okay. Move, please."

The rhythm they found together was instinctive, primal. She wrapped her legs around his waist, pulling him deeper, and he groaned against her neck.

"Maddie," he gasped. "My control...I can't..."

She looked up and saw what he meant. His eyes were fully gold now, glowing in the bedroom's darkness. His canines had lengthened slightly, and when his hands gripped her hips, she felt the sharp prick of his claws.

"It's okay, Nico," she whispered. "I'm not afraid."

"You should be. When the bond completes, when I claim you, it's going to be intense."

"Show me."

Something wild flashed in his eyes. He adjusted them both so that he was sitting up with her in his lap, her legs straddling his hips. This new angle was deeper, more intense, and she cried out.

"That's it," he growled, his voice rougher now, more bear than man. "Take what you need. Claim me back, Maddie."

They moved together, faster now, chasing release. Nico's mouth found the junction of her neck and shoulder, and she felt his teeth. Sharp but careful, as they pressed against her skin.

"Mine," he growled. "Say it. Say you're mine."

"Yours," she gasped. "I'm yours, Nico. Always."

His teeth sank in, not deep enough to truly hurt, but enough to mark, to claim. At the same moment, she felt something snap into place, like a door opening in her chest. She could feel him, not just physically but emotionally. His love, need, and his absolute certainty that she belonged to him.

The mate bond.

It was overwhelming. Maddie shattered. "Nico!" she cried out his name as pleasure crashed over her. Nico followed moments later, roaring his release, his body shuddering as he held her tight.

They collapsed together, breathing hard, still joined. Maddie could feel his heart hammering against her chest, could feel their bond humming with satisfaction and love.

"Okay?" he asked, his voice hoarse.

"That was..." She couldn't find words. "Wow."

He laughed, the sound rumbling through his chest. "Yeah, wow."

He pulled back to look at her, and his eyes were still golden but softer now, sated. "You're marked. Everyone will know you're mine now."

She touched her neck, feeling the slight tenderness where his teeth had pressed. "Good."

"Good?"

"I want them to know. I want everyone to know I'm yours." She pushed him back onto the bed and straddled him again. "My turn."

His eyes widened. "Maddie—"

"You claimed me, now I'm claiming you back."

What followed was slower, more exploratory. Maddie took her time learning every inch of him, discovering what made him gasp and groan. When he was trembling beneath her, barely holding on to control, she leaned down and bit his shoulder. Not as hard as he'd bitten her, but with intention, claiming.

"Mine," she said fiercely. "You're mine, Nico Matthews. My mate, my love. Mine."

The bond flared brighter, and she felt his emotions crash over her: pride, love, and possessive satisfaction as she claimed him as well.

She collapsed next to him, snuggled into the curve of his arm, and let out a deep breath. His body heat alone was enough to keep her warm. This is what she wanted out of life. The love she already felt between them is what she'd sought all her life.

"Sarah mentioned something to me." He dragged his fingers along the curve of her hip.

"What's that?"

"She thought you might be willing to put your event planning skills to use for this town." He paused for a moment before adding. "You said that life didn't make you happy, so if you're not interested, she'll understand."

"I need to find work." She tipped her head up at him. "I enjoy event planning, and I'm good at it. It wasn't the work that didn't bring me joy, it was the corporate grind of it all."

"So why not start your own business?" he suggested. "The town's looking for someone to organize festivals, weddings, and community events. There are also businesses in the area that might need help. I know you could help me plan some stuff around here for next year's Christmas. At the tree farm, we used to have stalls selling homemade baked goods and artisan items. I want to bring it back."

"I could do that. I love to use my skills for something more meaningful than corporate events."

"Whatever you want. We'll figure it out." He pulled her closer. "Stay here, in this house, with Oakley and me. Make this your home."

"Are you asking me to move in?"

"I'm asking you to stay. Permanently. As my mate, as Oakley's..." He hesitated. "She needs a mother figure. Someone who can teach her things I can't, guide her through growing up as a young shifter female. I know it's a lot to ask—"

"Yes."

"I don't want to pressure you into...wait, yes?"

"Yes, I'll stay, and I'll be here for Oakley. Yes, to all of it. We're together for everything." She propped herself up to look at him. "I love that little girl, and I'd be honored to help raise her."

The relief and love in his expression made her eyes sting with tears.

"Thank you," he whispered. "For choosing us, for staying, and for being exactly what we needed."

"You're what I needed too. Both of you." She kissed him softly. "I came here broken and lost, and you made me whole again."

"We made each other whole."

Wrapped in his arms, listening to his steady heartbeat, Maddie thought about the journey that had brought her here. Losing her job, breaking up with Derek, and renting a cabin on a whim from a woman she didn't even know. Every wrong turn, every disappointment, every moment of pain had led her here. To this man, his family, and his clan. To this impossible, wonderful life.

"Merry Christmas," Nico murmured against her hair as the sky began to lighten with dawn.

"Merry Christmas," she whispered back.

Outside, the first snowflakes of Christmas morning began to fall, blanketing the world in fresh white. Inside, in the warmth of Nico's arms, Maddie finally understood what coming home really meant.

CHAPTER 18
HOME FOR CHRISTMAS

Maddie woke to soft light filtering through unfamiliar windows and the steady rhythm of Nico's heartbeat next to her ear. For a moment, she just lay there, breathing him in. The pine, spice, and woodsmoke were so uniquely him. His arm was wrapped around her waist, holding her close even in sleep, and she could feel the mate bond humming contentedly between them.

She was marked. Claimed. His. Most importantly, she'd never been happier.

Through the window, she could see snow falling softly, blanketing the world in fresh white. Christmas morning had arrived quietly like a gift.

Nico stirred beneath her, his hand sliding up her back. "Morning," he rumbled, his voice rough with sleep.

"Merry Christmas."

"Best Christmas I've had in years." He pulled her up for a kiss, slow and sweet. "How do you feel?"

"Sore, happy, and a little overwhelmed." She touched the mark on her neck. Tender but already healing with shifter speed she acquired through their mate bond.

"Any regrets?" His eyes were warm amber in the morning light.

"Not a single one."

"Good, because you're stuck with me now."

"I can think of worse fates."

They kissed again when a door slammed downstairs, followed by rapid footsteps, and Oakley's excited voice echoed through the house.

"It's Christmas! Santa came! Wake up, wake up!"

Nico groaned. "I forgot about the six a.m. wake-up calls."

"Better get dressed then."

They threw on clothes quickly, with Maddie tossing one of Nico's flannels on along with her jeans. Her thoroughly wrinkled sweater was discarded on the floor and forgotten in the heat of their mating. When she caught sight of herself in his mirror, she froze.

The mark on her neck was visible above the collar of the shirt. Not quite a bruise or a bite, something in between that clearly said *claimed* to anyone who knew what to look for.

"Everyone's going to know," she said.

"Everyone already knew." Nico came up behind her, wrapping his arms around her waist. "Shifters can smell the mate bond. They've known since the festival. This just makes it official."

"What will they think?"

"That their alpha is happy for the first time in four years. That Oakley has someone who loves her, and the clan has a new member who's already proven she belongs here." He kissed her temple. "They'll think what I think that we're lucky to have you."

A louder knock came at the door. "Daddy! Miss Maddie! Are you awake? Santa came, and there are so many presents, and Aunt Lucia is already making pancakes."

Nico called through the door, "We're awake, sweetie. Give us two minutes."

"Okay, but hurry. Christmas is waiting!"

They heard her thundering back down the stairs.

"Ready?" Nico asked, taking Maddie's hand.

"Ready."

They went downstairs together, hand in hand, to find Oakley practically vibrating with excitement in front of the Christmas tree. She was still in her red pajamas with the snowflakes. Her hair was wild from sleep, but her face was flushed with pure joy.

Oakley stopped bouncing when she saw them, and her eyes widened.

"Miss Maddie!" She looked at Maddie, then at their joined hands, then at her dad. "Did you...are you...is Miss Maddie staying?"

"Maddie?" he said gently.

Oakley's gaze focused on her. "Miss Maddie?"

Maddie knelt to Oakley's level, her heart full. "If you'll have me, I'm staying forever."

Oakley launched herself at Maddie, wrapping her arms around her neck. "Yes! This is the best Christmas present ever."

Maddie held her tight, feeling tears sting her eyes. Over Oakley's head, she met Nico's gaze and saw the same emotion reflected there: love, gratitude, and wonder that this was their life now.

"Does this mean you're going to be my new mom?" Oakley asked, pulling back just enough to look at Maddie's face.

"I..." Maddie glanced up at Nico, uncertain how to answer.

"It means that Maddie is going to live here with us," Nico explained. "She and I are mates now, and she's part of our family."

"So, she's like a mom, but we call her Maddie?"

"If that's what she wants," Nico said.

"What do you want?" Oakley asked Maddie.

Maddie thought about the weight of that title and about Elena's photo on the dresser, and the mother Oakley barely remembered.

"How about we start with Maddie and see what feels right as we go?" she suggested. "I'm not trying to replace your mama, but I'm here for you, always. Whatever you need, whatever you want to call me, I'm here."

Oakley seemed to consider this, then nodded thoughtfully.

"Okay, but I think I'd like to call you Mom if that's okay. Because even though I don't remember my first mom very much, I think she'd want me to have someone, and I want that someone to be you."

"I would be honored." Maddie's eyes prickled with grateful tears.

"Okay, good." Oakley's mood instantly brightened. "Now, can we please open presents? I've been waiting forever!"

Lucia appeared from the kitchen, spatula in hand, grinning at the scene. "Merry Christmas, you disgustingly happy people. Maddie, that's quite a mark you've got there."

Maddie's hand flew to her neck. "I—"

"Relax, I'm teasing. It's about time my brother claimed his mate officially." She pointed the spatula at Nico. "Though you could have waited until I left. The walls in this house are not as thick as you think."

"Lucia," Nico growled warningly.

"What? I'm just saying—"

"Aunt Lucia, presents!" Oakley interrupted. "We can talk about gross adult stuff later."

"You're right. Presents first." Lucia headed back to the kitchen. "Pancakes in ten minutes. Make it quick."

The next hour was pure joy. Oakley opened presents with enthusiastic abandon. She was excited about everything she got, from the new books to art supplies to clothes to a beautiful wooden dollhouse that Nico had spent months making. She insisted on opening presents for Maddie, too, even though Maddie protested she hadn't expected gifts.

But there were gifts. A beautiful wool scarf from Lucia. A collection of local history books from Kate, with a note: *Welcome to Timber Ridge. Now you're part of our story.* There was even a small carved bear from Oakley that she'd apparently made in art class.

"So, you always remember us," Oakley explained. "At least that's why I decided to give that to you. But now you're staying forever, so you won't need to remember us because you'll always be here."

"It's perfect," Maddie said, running her thumb over the carved wood. "I'll treasure it always."

Nico's gift was last, a delicate silver necklace with a small pendant. When Maddie looked closer, she realized it was engraved with coordinates.

"The exact location where we met," he explained quietly. "The cabin where everything changed."

"Nico," she breathed. "It's beautiful."

"Let me." He reached out, taking the necklace from her and fastening it around her neck. His fingers lingered on the mark he'd left there. "So, you always remember where we started."

"I could never forget." She caressed the edges of the pendant as her lips curled up into a smile.

The snow was still falling by the time the clan started to arrive. Marcus and his wife were first, bearing cookies and a bottle of wine. Sarah, her husband, and her baby were almost right behind them. It wasn't long before the house was fuller than the night before. Yet, it wasn't overwhelming, it was comforting. Warmth and laughter filled the space.

"Our alpha's mate," Grayson said, shaking her hand with genuine warmth. "Officially, this time. Congratulations and welcome to the family."

"Thank you for accepting me."

"You accepted us first. Not everyone could handle learning about shifters and still choose to stay. That takes courage."

Throughout the afternoon, people pulled her aside with similar sentiments. Sarah hugged her and whispered, "Oakley won't stop talking about you. Thank you for making her so happy."

"Can you hold her?" Sarah asked, handing off the baby before she could answer. "I'm starving, and she hates to be put down."

"Analisa got used to being held because everyone in the clan wanted to hold her as a baby." Nico came up beside her, looking down at the small child in her arms.

"Well, why not? She's adorable and so well behaved."

"You haven't seen her at two in the morning," Sarah called from the table where food was spread out.

She gently rocked Analisa in her arms when Lee stepped into the house. His gaze shot between everyone, and she could see he wanted to run. She understood it was a little overwhelming, but if he was going to be part of the clan, he needed to accept this. She stepped away from the others, moving slowly toward him, as he still lingered at the door.

"Lee." She kept her voice low, not to frighten him further.

"Uh...you know me?"

"Yes...well, no, we haven't officially met."

"Lee, this is my mate, Maddie." Nico came up beside her. "I'm glad you joined us. Come on in. Get something to eat."

"I..." With wide eyes, he looked around at all of them gathered in the house.

"It's okay, Lee. This is your clan now. Family. No one here is going to hurt you," she encouraged.

"Come on, I'll introduce you to some of the others." Nico tilted his head toward the crowd. "You already know Grayson."

Lee swallowed before nodding. "Okay."

"I'm glad you're here." She looked at the young kid and wanted to wrap her arms around him and promise him everything would be fine. But she kept her hands to herself and watched as Nico led him toward a couple of members near Lee's age.

Sarah had finished eating, and Maddie made her way through the crowd to hand Analisa back.

"You're a natural. You'll do great when you have your own," Sarah whispered as she took the now sleeping baby back.

The thought sent a thrill through her. Having children with Nico, giving Oakley siblings, and watching their family grow around them.

"I'm glad you accepted all of this," Kate said, making Maddie turn around. "Elena would have liked you. She would have wanted this for Nico and Oakley. She would have wanted them to be happy again."

Tears pricked Maddie's eyes. "Thank you for saying that."

"Welcome home, dear. You've always belonged here. You just had to find your way to us."

As the sun set on Christmas day and the last guests departed, Maddie stood at the window watching snow falling over the mountains. Nico came up behind her, wrapping his arm around her waist.

"Tired?" he asked.

"Exhausted, happy, and maybe a little overwhelmed."

"Too much?"

"No." She leaned back against him. "It's perfect. They're all perfect. This is perfect."

"Daddy! Maddie! Come watch the movie with me," Oakley called from the sofa where she'd set up camp with blankets and pillows.

"She's going to be calling you Mom within a week," Nico murmured.

"I know." Maddie turned in his arms. "Is that okay? Is it too soon?"

"Elena would have wanted it, and I want whatever makes Oakley happy. Whatever makes you happy."

"You make me happy. Both of you."

They joined Oakley on the sofa, Maddie in the middle with Nico on one side and Oakley curled against her other side. Some animated Christmas movie played on the television, but Maddie barely watched it. She was too busy soaking in the moment. The warmth of the house, the peace of being surrounded by family, and the absolute rightness of where she was.

Halfway through the movie, Oakley fell asleep against Maddie's shoulder, her breathing deep and even.

"She's out," Nico whispered.

"Should we move her to bed?"

"In a minute." He kissed Maddie's temple. "I want to remember this. The three of us on our first Christmas together."

"The first of many," Maddie said softly.

"The first of many," he agreed.

Lucia appeared in the doorway, overnight bag in hand. "I'm heading out. Got a long drive back to the city."

"It's getting late, you should stay the night."

"You guys deserve some family time without me in the way." She smiled at the scene on the sofa. "Besides, I have my own life to figure out. Watching you two has been...inspiring in a nauseating, overly romantic kind of way."

"Lucia—"

"I'm happy for you, Nico. Really. You deserve this, all of it." She looked at Maddie. "Take care of them and welcome to the family, officially."

"Drive safely." Maddie nodded.

Lucia strolled out the door, and Nico lifted Oakley before carrying her up to bed. Maddie followed, helping tuck her in and smoothing back her hair.

"Best Christmas ever," Oakley mumbled, half-asleep. "Love you both."

"Love you too, sweetheart," Maddie whispered.

They stepped out of her room and headed to Nico's room, not their room, and got ready for bed in comfortable silence. When

Maddie climbed under the covers, Nico pulled her close, the mating bond humming contentedly between them.

"Thank you." He nuzzled against her neck.

"For what?"

"For showing up, for staying, and for giving us a second chance at being a family."

"Thank you for taking a chance on me and for seeing past the mess I was when I got here."

"You were never a mess. You were finding your way home."

And as Maddie drifted off to sleep in Nico's arms, snow still falling softly outside, and the house quiet and peaceful around them, she knew it was true. She'd found her way home. Finally.

EPILOGUE

Six Months Later

S pring had come to the mountains in an explosion of green and gold.

Maddie stood at the kitchen window of the main house, her house now. Wildflowers blanket the meadow where snow had been just weeks ago. The aspens were leafing out, their new growth bright against the dark pines. Birds sang from every branch. The world felt alive, renewed, full of possibility. Just like her.

She touched her stomach, still flat beneath her loose shirt, and smiled at the secret she carried.

Two pink lines. She'd taken the test that morning while Nico was out on patrol and Oakley was still at Emma's. She'd stared at them for a full minute, her heart racing, before the joy had crashed over her.

Pregnant. She was pregnant with Nico's child.

The mate bond had hummed with her emotions, and she'd felt Nico's confusion from across the property. Felt him trying to figure out why she was suddenly radiating such intense happiness mixed with nervousness. She'd consciously damped her feelings through their bond, saving the news for when she could tell him in person.

Even now that he was nearby, she waited to tell him the news. "Tonight, I'll tell him tonight, after Oakley goes to bed."

It had taken Oakley exactly six days after Christmas to start calling Maddie "Mom." She seemed nervous about it, but when tears filled Maddie's eyes, Oakley threw her arms around her and whispered, "I think my first mom sent you to us. I think she knew we needed you."

Now, *Mom* was as natural as breathing. Maddie helped with homework and braided hair, which Oakley said was much better than Nico's attempt. She attended parent-teacher conferences and school plays. She was even teaching Oakley to bake and answering questions about growing up and being there for all the small, important moments that made up a childhood.

She was Oakley's mom, and soon she'd be mom to another little one. The very thought made her giddy and terrified in equal measure.

The front door opened, and Lucia breezed in carrying grocery bags. "I'm back, and I brought you the chocolate you like. The fancy dark chocolate with the sea salt. Pregnant women need chocolate. Sarah told me horror stories about her cravings."

Maddie's eyes went wide. "How did you—"

"Please, I'm a shifter. Remember? I could smell the change in you the second I arrived yesterday." Lucia set down the bags and grinned. "Plus, you've been wearing loose shirts and turned practically green when I mentioned eggs this morning. Not exactly subtle."

"Does Nico know?"

"Your mate is many things, but observant about subtle human pregnancy signs is not one of them. He's been too busy being disgustingly happy to notice you've been sneaking crackers and avoiding strong smells." Lucia pulled Maddie into a hug. "Congratulations. I'm going to be an aunt again."

"I haven't told him yet."

"Then I won't either. But Maddie, he's going to be thrilled. And Oakley is going to lose her mind with excitement."

Lucia now visits regularly, staying in the main house instead of the cabin on weekends or during long holiday breaks. The relationship between her and Nico had slowly healed over the past months. Tentative at first, then growing stronger. They'd never be the siblings they were before their parents' deaths, but they were finding a new way to be family.

Maddie had helped with that, serving as a bridge between them, reminding Nico to listen and Lucia to be patient. She encouraged them both to continue working to build their relationship because family was everything.

"How's the city?" Maddie asked, helping Lucia unpack groceries.

"Loud, crowded, and expensive." Lucia smiled. "But it's where I need to be right now. I may be up for a promotion. I'm being considered for partnership at the law firm."

"That's wonderful!"

"Thanks. Though I have to admit, coming back here is getting easier. Less suffocating." She glanced out the window at Nico and Oakley. "You've been good for him, for both of them. Really, for all of us. You remind us that family doesn't have to be a cage."

"Family is whatever you make it," Maddie said softly.

"Exactly." Lucia squeezed her shoulder. "Okay, enough sappy stuff. Tell me about the wedding you're planning. Sarah said it's going to be the event of the season."

Maddie's event planning business had taken off faster than she'd expected. As it happened, a tucked-away mountain town full of tradition-loving shifters, in desperate need of someone to plan their celebrations, was the perfect market for her skillset.

She planned three anniversary parties, two weddings, a baby shower, and was currently organizing the town's spring festival. She worked from home, set her own hours, and used her creativity for events that actually mattered to the people involved.

It was everything her old corporate job hadn't been. Meaningful, flexible, and fulfilling. It also left her plenty of time for the things that mattered most: family dinners with Nico and Oakley, lazy Sunday mornings in bed with her mate, long walks in the mountains, and being present for all the small moments that made up life.

"Mom!" Oakley's voice rang out from the yard. "Come see what we planted."

"Coming," Maddie called back.

She headed outside, with Lucia following. The afternoon sun was warm on her face, the air sweet with the scent of fresh earth.

Nico looked up as she approached, his gaze immediately finding hers, the mate bond sending a wave of love washing over her. Six months together, and that look still made her heart race.

"Look." Oakley gestured proudly to the freshly planted row. "We planted carrots, tomatoes, and green beans. Dad said in the fall, we can plant pumpkins for Halloween."

"It looks perfect," Maddie said, kneeling to examine their work.

"Over here is going to be my fairy garden." Oakley pointed to a small plot near the house. "We're going to plant tiny flowers and make little houses and everything."

"That sounds magical."

"It will be! Dad says we can start it next weekend. Will you help?"

"I'd love to."

Oakley beamed and ran off to wash her hands at the outdoor spigot.

He came closer, brushing a kiss against her temple. Through the bond, she felt his contentment and his satisfaction with the life they'd built.

"You're happy," he observed.

"I'm very happy."

"Good. That's all I want. For you and Oakley to be happy." He pulled her closer, his hands settling on the small of her back. "Though you've been feeling...different today. Through the bond. Excited about something."

160

"Maybe I am."

"Want to tell me about it?"

"Tonight," she promised. "After Oakley goes to bed. I have something I want to talk to you about."

His eyes searched her face, and concern pulled the corners of his eyes tight. "Is everything okay?"

"Everything is perfect." She kissed him softly. "I promise."

He relaxed, and the simple faith in that trust made her eyes sting with happy tears. This impossible, wonderful man who had given her a family, a home, and a future she'd never imagined wanting.

"Okay, lovebirds." Lucia cleared her throat meaningfully. "Some of us are single and don't need to watch the googly eyes. Oakley! Want to help me make dinner?"

"Yes." Oakley ran over, grinning. "Can we make spaghetti with a really good sauce?"

"We can make whatever you want, kiddo. Come on."

After they went inside, Nico pulled Maddie back against his chest, wrapping his arms around her waist. They stood there in the garden, watching the sun paint the mountains gold.

"I love you," he murmured against his hair.

"I love you too."

"I can't believe you've only been here six months. It feels like you've always been here."

"I know. I feel the same. This is home." Maddie placed her hands over his, where they rested on her stomach, right over the tiny life growing there, the future they'd created together.

She thought about the woman who had arrived in Timber Ridge months ago, heartbroken, unemployed, and directionless. Running from a life that had fallen apart, with no idea what came next. She'd been so lost and broken.

Now look at her. She had a home filled with love and laughter. She had a family, a mate who cherished her, a daughter who needed her, and a community that had welcomed her with open arms. She had a purpose, work that fulfilled her, and friends who'd become like family. Soon, she'd have another child. Another piece of this impossible, wonderful life.

"What are you thinking about?" Nico asked.

"About how I came here broken and lost," she said softly. "About how you and Oakley put me back together and how sometimes the worst things that can happen to you lead you exactly where you're supposed to be."

"And where's that?"

"Here, with you and Oakley. With all of this." She squeezed his hands. "This is where I was always meant to be."

"Then it's a good thing you're terrible at leaving."

She laughed and turned in his arms. "Remember that first night when you told me I couldn't stay?"

"My worst decision ever."

"I thought you were so arrogant and controlling."

"I was terrified," he admitted. "My bear knew what you were the second I saw you, and I was terrified of feeling that way again. Of risking my heart and letting someone in."

"Now?"

"Now, I can't imagine my life without you in it." He kissed her forehead before working down to her lips. "You're my mate, my love, and my second chance at happiness. I thank whatever force in the universe led you to that cabin, to me."

"Me too," she whispered.

The future stretched ahead, full of possibility and promise. Maddie Garrett, now Maddie Matthews, was ready for all of it.

She'd come to Timber Ridge running from her old life, and she found everything she never knew she needed. A mate, family, and a future. Love in all its forms.

"Come on," she said, taking Nico's hand. "Let's go have dinner with our family. Later, when Oakley's asleep, I'll tell you my secrets."

"Can I get a hint?"

She smiled and placed his hand over her still flat stomach. "Just know that our family is about to get a little bigger."

She felt understanding dawn on him through the bond. His shock, joy, and overwhelming love crashed over her like a wave.

"Maddie," he breathed. "Are you..."

"Yes."

He swept her up into his arms, spinning her around, his laugh echoing across the mountains. Through the window, she could see Oakley watching, confused, but smiling.

"We're having a baby," Nico said, his eyes glowing gold with emotion. "We're having a baby!"

He kissed her, deep and claiming, and the mate bond sang between them with joy, love, and perfect contentment.

This was what happiness felt like. Not the absence of problems or challenges. But love was messy, real, complicated, and wonderful.

The kind worth fighting for. The kind worth believing in, even when it seemed impossible.

As they walked back into the house hand in hand, ready to start the next chapter of their lives together, Maddie looked back once at the mountains. At the place that had saved her, and smiled, because she was exactly where she was meant to be. *Home.*

PREVIEW: CARVED IN TIMBER RIDGE

She came home searching for answers. She found her destiny instead.

Aleece Reeves never quite belonged anywhere, not in the shifter town that raised her, and not in the human world where she went to college. As the adopted human daughter of Timber Ridge's mayor, she's spent her whole life caught between two worlds. Now, graduated from college, she's back home for good, and more lost than ever.

When bear shifter Charles Monroe shows up to fix her father's burst pipes on a freezing January morning, the instant connection between them takes her breath away. Charles is everything she didn't know she needed: patient, kind, and building his dream home with his own two hands. Working alongside him on his renovation project, she finally feels like she's found where she belongs.

Just as Aleece begins to imagine a future in Timber Ridge and with Charles, her biological father appears, bringing devastating truths about her past. Now she must choose between life in the city and the terrifying possibility of loving a bear shifter who could break her heart.

Sometimes the bravest choice isn't running away, it's standing still and building something that lasts.

CHAPTER ONE:
COMING HOME

T he town limit sign appeared through the light snow flurries like an old friend waving hello. Aleece eased off the gas pedal, slowing as she took in the familiar sight. *Home.*

The word should have brought comfort, but instead, her stomach twisted with an uncomfortable mix of relief and dread. She'd been making this drive every weekend for four years and knew every curve of the mountain road, but this time was different. This time, she was finally moving back home. It had been four long years, but this time, as she drove into town, she was a returning resident, not a visitor.

The thought made her grip the steering wheel tighter as she navigated down Main Street. Timber Ridge looked picture-perfect in the winter afternoon light. It was the kind of small mountain town that belonged on a postcard. Storefronts lined both sides of the street, their awnings dusted with fresh snow. Warm lights glowed from the shop windows already decorated for Valentine's Day, though it was only mid-January. Mrs. Appleton was hanging a new sign at the diner. Ricky was shoveling the sidewalk in front of his dad's hardware store, his breath forming clouds in the cold air.

He looked up as she passed, raising his shovel in greeting. She waved back automatically, her chest tightening. Everyone knew her here. They'd watched her grow up, asked about college every time she came home for the weekend. They'd all be asking about her plans now, about what came next. The problem was, she didn't have an answer.

Aleece turned into the residential area where she'd grown up. The houses were older, well-maintained, with large yards and that established feel that came from generations of families putting down roots. She'd always loved the neighborhood. The way the neighbors actually talked to each other, kids still played outside even in the winter, and the way everyone looked out for each other. But lately, she'd started to wonder if that closeness was comforting or suffocating.

Her father's house came into view. A two-story craftsman with a wide front porch and a porch swing where she'd spent countless summer evenings. The sight of it made her throat tight. Her father, Mayor Thomas Reeves, had already shoveled the driveway and scattered salt on the walkway. The light by the door was on even though the sun wasn't down, a beacon welcoming her home.

She pulled into the driveway and shut off the engine, sitting for a moment in the sudden silence. Through the front window, she could see movement. Dad was likely watching for her and probably had been for the past hour, knowing him.

The front door opened before she could even grab her purse. Dad stepped onto the porch, and the smile on his face made her eyes sting with unexpected tears. He was a big man with broad shoulders and kind eyes that crinkled at the corners. His dark hair was graying at the temples. She wasn't certain when that had happened.

"There's my girl," he called out, already heading down the steps despite the cold. He wasn't wearing a coat, just his usual sweater and jeans. Shifters ran hot. The January chill didn't bother him the way it did her.

She climbed out of the car, and before she could say anything, he had pulled her into one of his tight hugs. The kind that lifted her off her feet and squeezed the air from her lungs in the best way possible, while also making her feel safe and that everything would be okay.

"Hi, Dad," she mumbled against his shoulder, breathing in the familiar scent of him that reminded her of home.

"Welcome back, sweetheart." He set her down but kept his hand on her shoulders, studying her face. His smile faltered slightly. "You look tired."

"Six-hour drive," she deflected, but she knew that wasn't what he meant. The exhaustion went deeper than a long drive. It had been building for months. Through finals, the stress of graduation, and the slow realization that finishing college didn't magically provide her with answers about her future.

"Well, let's get you inside and warmed up. I made your favorite, beef stew. It has been simmering all day." Thomas grabbed two suitcases from her back seat like they weighed nothing. "We can unload the rest later."

"Dad, I can carry—"

"I know you can, but humor your old man."

She grabbed her backpack and followed him up the walk, her boots crunching on the salt crystals. The porch swing swayed slightly in the breeze, and she remembered sitting there a few months ago, telling her father about her classes and how she couldn't wait to be home for good.

Graduation had come and gone, but her lease hadn't been up until the fifteenth of January. She'd spent the holidays in Timber Ridge in a weird limbo. She was done with school but not quite home. All of the limbo gave her time to overthink her future.

Inside the house was exactly as she remembered, though the Christmas decorations that had been up when she went to pack her apartment were now down. Warm and cluttered in a comfortable way, with her father's collection of books on the shelves and photos covering every available surface. Photos of her first day of school, soccer games, prom, high school graduation, and most recently, college graduation. A whole life documented.

She set her backpack down by the stairs and stood in the entryway, suddenly overwhelmed by the weight of everything. This house, the town, and the life waiting for her. She'd wanted to come home so badly during college. She had counted down the days to each weekend visit. So why did she feel like she couldn't breathe now that she was here?

"Aleece?"

She blinked, realizing her father was watching her with concern. "Sorry, just...processing, I guess."

"It's a big change." He set her suitcase down at the base of the stairs. "But you've got time to adjust. No rush on anything."

Except she felt like there was a rush. She was twenty-two years old with a degree in business administration and no clear direction. She couldn't just live in her childhood bedroom indefinitely, working part-time at the diner as she had in high school.

"Go ahead and get settled," he said, his voice gentle. "Dinner will be ready soon. Your room is all made up."

She nodded, grabbed her backpack, and one of the suitcases. The stairs creaked in the familiar way as she climbed to the second floor. Her room was at the end of the hall. The same room she'd had since her father had brought her home as a baby.

She pushed open the door and had to smile despite the swirling thoughts. Her father had clearly been busy. The room was spotless, her bed made with fresh sheets, and there were fresh flowers, winter jasmine, her favorite, in the vase on the dresser.

Her bookshelf still held her childhood favorites alongside college textbooks. Her desk sat under the window that looked out over the backyard, the same desk where she'd done her homework, filled out college applications, and written countless papers during weekend visits home. Everything was the same, yet it was all so different at the same time.

She set her suitcase on the bed and moved to the window. The backyard was blanketed in snow, the old oak tree bare-branched against the gray sky. Beyond the fence, she could see the mountains that cradled Timber Ridge, their peaks disappearing into low clouds.

She'd missed this view. During college, she kept it in mind during every stressful moment, especially when she was homesick or felt like she didn't quite fit in with her classmates, who didn't understand why she went home every single weekend. But now that she was here, looking at it in person instead of in her memory, she felt uncertain. Trapped almost, but that wasn't quite right. Like the view was asking her a question, she didn't know how to answer.

A soft knock on the door made her turn, and her father stood there, hands in his pockets, with that concerned dad expression on his face.

"You okay, sweetheart?"

She forced a smile. "Yeah, just tired. Long day."

She could tell from the way his eyebrows pulled together that he didn't buy it, but he didn't push. That was one of the things she loved about him. He gave her space to figure things out on her own, but he was always there when she needed him.

"I've been meaning to ask," he said, leaning against the doorframe. "How's the job search going? You mentioned some applications the last time we talked."

There it was, the question she'd been dreading.

"I've um...I've applied to a few places." She turned back to her suitcase, unzipping it so she wouldn't have to look at him. "I sent my resume to the county office. They have an opening in the administrative office. I also sent it to the A-Z accounting here in town. I saw that Mr. Ross is looking for a business manager. I know I don't have the experience, but—"

"Both solid opportunities." His voice was warm with pride. "County jobs have good benefits, and Mr. Ross, you did your internship with him."

"Yeah." She pulled out a stack of sweaters, buying time. "I also applied to a couple of places in the city. Just...you know, keeping my options open."

The silence that followed was heavy. She risked a glance back at her father and saw that his expression had shifted. Still supportive, but with an underlying sadness that made her chest ache.

"The city," he repeated carefully. "That's a good idea. Cast a wide net."

"Dad—"

"No, really. You should explore all of your options. You worked hard for that degree and graduated with honors. You shouldn't limit yourself." He was trying so hard to sound encouraging, but she could hear the disappointment underneath.

She set the sweaters down and turned to face him fully. "I don't know what I want yet. I need to figure things out."

"Of course you do. You just graduated. Nobody expects you to have it all figured out right away." He crossed his arms over his broad chest. His version of keeping himself from reaching out to fix things. "But I need to ask, are you happy to be home? Or do you feel like you have to be here?"

The question hit harder than she expected. "I don't know," she admitted quietly. "I missed this place so much while I was at school. Every weekend I was here, I dreaded going back. But now that I'm here for good..." Her words trailed off, not sure how to finish.

"Now that you're here, it feels different," he finished for her.

"Yeah." Relief flooded through her that he understood. "Is that terrible? You took me in when nobody else wanted me, and you gave me everything. Yet, I'm standing here wondering if I can actually build a life in Timber Ridge."

He crossed the room and pulled her into a hug, gentler this time. "That's not terrible, it's honest. Aleece, you don't owe me anything. Not your whole life, not your future. I took you in because I wanted to. You needed a home, and I had one to give. That doesn't mean you're obligated to stay here forever."

She pressed her face against his shoulder, fighting back tears. "But what if I leave and I'm miserable? What if I stay and I'm miserable? How do I know which choice is right?"

"You don't. Not yet." He pulled back, cupping her face in his big hands. "But you've got time to figure it out. Send out those applications and see what happens. Maybe you'll get the perfect job here in town. Maybe you'll get an offer in the city that's too good to pass up. Or maybe something completely different will happen. Either way, you don't have to decide today."

She nodded, blinking back tears. "I'm scared I'll make the wrong choice."

"Then you'll make a different choice. That's the thing about life, sweetheart. Very few decisions are permanent." His smile was soft. "Except for adopting kids. That one's pretty permanent, but even that turned out pretty well."

Despite everything, she laughed. "Pretty well?"

"Okay, amazingly well. You turned out perfect." He kissed her forehead. "Now, come on. Let's eat. You can unpack later. Or tomorrow. Or next week. The suitcases aren't going anywhere."

Dinner was comfortable in a way that only came from years of shared meals. Dad ladled out generous portions of beef stew. All it took was one bite to remind her how delicious his cooking was. Throughout dinner, the conversation was easy. He filled her in on the town gossip. The clan alpha, Nico, found his mate at Christmas, and Maddie was making herself an essential part of the clan.

"Can you believe Maddie convinced me to have the town sponsor a Valentine's Day decorating contest? All the storefronts can enter by decorating their shopfronts, and residents will vote for their favorites."

"What's the prize?"

"Gift certificates to a bunch of stores in town, a beautiful handmade quilt donated by Kate from the general store. Then, each month this year, we're doing a different theme window display competition, with the town picking a winner each time. Then at the Christmas festival, we'll draw one final winner. We haven't announced the grand prize yet since some of it is still in the works." He shook his head. "Maddie and her event planning business have really taken off, but she's always got these great ideas for the community as well. I've asked her to help with the Christmas festival."

"Seems like she is the perfect mate for Nico." She brought a spoonful of beef stew to her lips before smirking.

"What's the smirk for?" he asked.

"Maddie isn't just good for Nico. Seems like she's got you wrapped around her little finger, too."

"How's that?"

"Really, Dad?" She took a piece of the fresh Italian bread he'd placed in the center of the table and buttered it. "Maddie's been here a month, and she's already got the town and the mayor doing more community engagement."

"Maddie and Nico also convinced the county to finally repave Main Street." He took a bite of the stew before glancing up at her. "I don't know how she does it, but she's very convincing. You can't say no to her."

"I see." She dunked her bread into the bowl, allowing it to soak up some of the delicious broth.

"So..." Dad's tone turned careful. "Any idea what you're looking for in a job? Besides a paycheck, I mean."

There it was. Just like that, the conversation turned serious. "I don't know. Something that matters. I didn't spend four years studying business just to push papers around."

"The county position would involve some community outreach," he offered. "Working with local programs and all sorts of things."

"Yeah, that could be good." She stared into her soup. "But the city jobs...they're with bigger companies. More room for advancement and better pay."

"Also, more hours, a longer commute, and a higher cost of living."

"I know." She sighed. "See? This is what I mean. Every option has pros and cons. How do people make these decisions?"

Thomas was quiet for a moment, then said, "Can I tell you something? You don't have to agree with me, but...hear me out."

"Of course." She looked up at him.

"When I was younger, I had opportunities to leave Timber Ridge. Good opportunities. There was a construction company in Denver that wanted to hire me, back before I went into politics. Big money, important projects." He leaned back in his chair, his gaze distant. "I turned them down because I knew, in my gut, that I belonged here. This town, these people, these mountains, they were my place, and I've never regretted that choice, not for a single day."

"But?" she prompted, sensing there was more.

"But that was *my* choice, based on what *I* needed. You're not me, sweetheart. You might need something different or somewhere different." His gaze found hers, serious but loving all at once. "Don't stay here because you think it's what I want. Don't stay here out of obligation or guilt. Stay because you can't imagine being anywhere else. Anything less than that, and you'll always wonder what if."

She felt her throat tighten. "What if I don't know? What if I can imagine being happy in both places?"

"Then you pick one and see what happens. If it doesn't work out, you'll figure something else out." He smiled. "You're twenty-two, Aleece. You've got time to make mistakes and change your mind."

She nodded, but the knot in her stomach didn't loosen. Time felt both infinite and terrifyingly short. She could spend years making the wrong choice before realizing it.

It was late, but Aleece couldn't sleep. Usually, when she had trouble sleeping, a nice hot cup of tea helped, but tonight she found herself with a mug of hot chocolate standing by the window looking out at the snow-covered neighborhood.

A few houses down, she could see the lights still on in the Patterson house. The teenage daughter was probably up late studying, just like Aleece used to do. Across the street, old Mr. Mason was out on his porch in his bathrobe, smoking his evening pipe despite the cold. He'd been doing that for as long as she could remember. Some things in Timber Ridge never changed.

She pressed her forehead against the cool glass. Four years ago, leaving for college had felt like an adventure. She'd been so ready to experience the world beyond Timber Ridge, to prove she could make it in the human world even though shifters raised her.

She'd made it. She'd gotten good grades, made friends, and learned to navigate a city where nobody knew her name. But she'd also been homesick in a way that felt like a physical ache. Every Friday afternoon, she would pack a bag and make the six-hour drive home, arriving just in time for dinner with her father. Every Sunday evening, she'd make the drive back, already counting down the days until she could return.

Her human friends had thought she was crazy. "Don't you want to stay for the parties?" they'd ask. "Don't you want to have a college experience?"

But they didn't understand. They had families they could call, siblings they could text, and parents who visited. Aleece only had her father, and he was in Timber Ridge. He'd come to Denver when she had something happening, but preferred to remain in Timber Ridge.

Except now she was there too, and the homesickness hadn't gone away. It had transformed into something else. A restless feeling that maybe she was supposed to be somewhere else, doing something else. Or maybe she was just tired and overthinking everything.

She pushed away from the window, set her mug of half-finished hot chocolate on the counter, and headed upstairs. Her suitcase still sat on her bed, half-unpacked. She should probably finish, put her clothes in drawers, and make the room feel like hers again.

Instead, she pulled out her laptop and opened her email. Three new messages: two automated responses from job applications and one from her friend Kathy from college, asking how the move went and demanding photos of the adorable small town. She ignored the messages and opened the search engine, but her cursor hovered over the search bar.

What am I looking for?

The question echoed in her mind, louder than it should have been at nearly one o'clock in the morning. She closed the laptop without searching for anything.

Tomorrow, she'd figure it out.

She finished unpacking mechanically, hanging clothes in her closet, lining up shoes, and setting her few framed photos on the dresser. Her college diploma, still in its cardboard tube, went on the desk. She'd frame it when she figured out what it was supposed to mean.

Finally, she climbed into bed, the same bed she'd slept in since she was five, when her father decided she should have a big girl bed. Instead of a twin-size mattress, they went shopping for one. She ended up with a huge full bed, because she was a princess and should have a big bed. It still had the same quilt Kate had made her for her sixteenth birthday, each square a different pattern coming together to be beautiful.

As she lay in bed, she could look out the window toward the mountain. They appeared just as dark shapes against the slightly light sky. Somewhere out there was the rest of the world. Cities and opportunities and futures she couldn't quite imagine. But here, in her room in her father's house, everything was familiar and safe.

She closed her eyes and tried not to feel like she was suffocating. She was home, and she should be happy. So why did happiness feel so far away?

PREVIEW: RETURN TO TIMBER RIDGE

Coming October 2026

She ran from control. He ran from pain. Together, they'll learn that home is worth the risk.
 Lucia Matthews left Timber Ridge at eighteen and never looked back. As a corporate lawyer weeks from making partner, she's built a life on one principle: never let anyone control you again. Until her pregnant sister-in-law's crisis pulls her home and she meets Kory.

Kory Denton is a man with ghosts. Following the death of his mate, he's been on the run and never looked back. After Christmas, he's gone. That's the plan.

But the mate bond has other ideas. An unexpected stay on a Christmas tree farm ignites something neither can ignore. Lucia's life crumbles as she's forced to choose between partnership or presence, career or connection. Kory's walls crack when a stubborn lawyer refuses to let him push her away.

Between a law firm demanding everything, a seven-year-old who needs her mother, and a broken shifter ready to heal, Lucia must

179

decide what she's really running toward. Kory must decide if he's brave enough to stop running and start living.

CHAPTER ONE:
THE WEEKLY DRIVE

The Denver skyline was disappearing in Lucia's rearview mirror when her phone rang. The dashboard lit up, displaying the last name she wanted to see right now: *Richard.*

"Of course," she muttered.

Technically off the clock, Lucia considered letting it go to voicemail, but associates who wanted to make partner didn't ignore senior partners. Even on Friday afternoons, when they were an hour into a six-hour drive to Timber Ridge.

"Lucia Matthews," she answered, keeping her voice bright and energized despite her annoyance.

"Where are you?" Richard Nickles' tone was clipped, impatient. "I called your office, and your assistant said you'd left already."

"I'm heading to Timber Ridge for the weekend for a family visit. I mentioned it in Monday's meeting."

"Right...your brother." There was a pause, loaded with disapproval. "Third weekend this month."

"Second," Lucia corrected, though she knew it wouldn't matter.

She merged onto the highway, heading into the mountains. "I'll have my laptop, if something urgent comes up."

"The Cannon's case *is* urgent. Depositions start next week, and we're not ready."

Lucia bit back a response. They were absolutely ready. She'd spent the past two weeks preparing. Every document was organized, and every witness was prepared, but Richard didn't like to be contradicted, even when he was wrong. He was a senior partner who took her under his wing and held the ticket to her promotion.

"I'll review the files again this weekend," she said instead. "If you need me to come back Sunday night instead of Monday morning—"

"What I need is for you to be in the office. Present and committed." His voice sharpened. "Partnership vote is in six months, Lucia. The other partners are watching. These weekend trips to the mountains don't scream dedication."

There it was, the warning she'd been expecting for weeks.

Her hands tightened on the steering wheel. "I've billed more hours than anyone else in my class. The Cannon case is solid. I haven't missed a deadline or a meeting—"

"But you're not here. You're always one foot out the door, heading back to that tiny town." He sighed, and she could picture him in his corner office, looking out over the city with that expression of vague disappointment he wore so well. "Look, I'm not trying to be the bad guy. I'm trying to help you. Partnership means sacrifice. It means putting the firm first. If you're not prepared to do that..."

He let the implication hang.

She stared at the highway stretching ahead, winding into the mountains. Six months ago, even six weeks ago, she'd have immediately reassured him of her commitment to this job. Would have promised to cancel her trips, to be in the office more, and to make whatever sacrifices it took. But that was before Christmas. Before Maddie and Oakley. Before learning what it felt like to be part of her family instead of running from it. Now she wasn't sure that the sacrifice was worth it.

"I understand," she said finally. "I'll call you tomorrow to discuss the Cannon prep."

"See that you do." He hung up without saying goodbye.

She exhaled slowly, forcing her shoulders to relax. The city was far behind her now, as the landscape shifted to pine forest and rocky cliffs. The late afternoon sun painted everything gold and amber. Despite Richard's warning, she felt some of the tension ease from her chest.

This drive had become familiar over the past few months. After Maddie and Nico's wedding in January, Lucia had started coming back to Timber Ridge more regularly. At first, it was only once a month, and it was full of uncertainties. Slowly, that turned into every other weekend, and now she was making the trip almost weekly. Each time, she was pulled to it by something she couldn't quite name, or maybe she was afraid to name it.

Her phone buzzed with a text message, and as she came to a red light, she glanced at the screen. Maddie.

> Are you close? I know you said around seven, but I'm hoping you'll be here soon. Having a rough day.

Lucia frowned and typed back one-handed.

> About two hours out. Everything okay?

> Fine. Just tired. Ignore me. Drive safely. Love you.

The casual *love you* still caught Lucia off guard sometimes. Maddie said it so easily, like it was the most natural thing in the world. Like Lucia had always been part of the family instead of the sister who'd run away at eighteen and barely looked back for a decade.

That was changing now. Slowly and carefully, she and Nico were rebuilding what had broken between them after their parents died. It wasn't easy. There was far too much history and too many years of resentment and misunderstandings, but they were trying.

Having Maddie as a sister-in-law helped. Maddie, who witnessed all the Matthew family dysfunction and somehow decided to stay anyway. Who'd claimed her mate bond with Nico and brought light back into his life.

Lucia pressed down on the accelerator, speeding up slightly.

The miles passed in a blur of pine trees and mountain peaks. She'd grown up in these mountains and knew every curve of this road. Nico had taught her to drive on the switchbacks, and as a teenager, she learned to shift in these forests. Then she'd left it all behind.

Her parents' deaths had shattered everything. Nico, only twenty-two then, had suddenly become the alpha of their clan and her guardian. He had tried to hold everything together. Suddenly, her brother was trying to be her parent, alpha, and brother all at once. He'd suffocated her with rules, expectations, and protective instincts.

The day after she turned eighteen, she was on the road to Denver. Thanks to her parents pushing her to dual-enroll in college classes while still in high school, she'd already completed three years of her undergrad and was accepted into a hybrid program. She'd finish the last year of her bachelor's while starting law school.

Denver seemed like the perfect place for a fresh start. Freedom. She'd built a life that was entirely hers, where nobody expected her to be anything except excellent. It wasn't until recently that she realized excellent also meant lonely.

But lately, driving away from the city had felt more like freedom than moving toward it. She shook off the thought. She had a good life, a career many would kill for, and a great condo with a view. She was respected, successful, and independent. She just wished it felt like enough.

Her phone rang again as she crossed into the town limits. This time, though, it wasn't Richard, it was her brother, Nico.

"Hey," she answered. "I'm literally pulling into town right now."

"Perfect." Her brother's voice was strained. "Are you coming straight to the house?"

Lucia's stomach sank. "What's wrong? Is Maddie—"

"She's fine, so is the baby. She's just..." He exhaled roughly. "Morning sickness has been brutal. She can't keep anything down, and she won't admit she needs help. Oakley's picking up on the stress and acting out. I've got three dozen things that need to happen at the farm before the season starts, and I—" He stopped abruptly.

She had never heard her brother sound so overwhelmed. Nico, who'd been alpha since he was barely more than a kid, had raised Oakley alone after Elena died and carried every responsibility like it was his sacred duty.

"Hold on, Nico, I'm ten minutes away."

She ended the call and drove faster than she should have through Main Street, past the general store where Kate waved from the window, past the diner, the small post office, and the town square with its massive pine tree. She always thought the town looked like something from a postcard. Quaint, cozy, and exactly the kind of place tourists paid good money to visit.

This place used to feel like a prison. Now it felt like...

She refused to finish the thought.

At the end of a long, winding driveway, the main house came into view. Smoke curled from the chimney despite the mild October weather. Nico's truck was parked at an angle, as if he'd been in a hurry to get inside. The Christmas tree farm stretched out behind the house, its rows and rows of evergreens waiting for the season to begin.

She grabbed her overnight bag from the passenger seat and headed for the front door. It opened before her high-heeled boots touched the wooden porch.

Nico looked like he hadn't slept in days. His dark hair was disheveled, his shirt wrinkled, and there were shadows under his amber eyes that hadn't been there last weekend.

"I'm so glad you're here," he said.

The statement was direct, but it was the first time in fifteen years her brother had said it and actually meant it. She felt a part deep within her break open. It had been locked tight for too long, and that statement was the final piece to crack it.

"Where do you need me?" she asked.

He sagged slightly with relief. "Everywhere."

From inside the house, Oakley hollered, her voice high and anxious, "Daddy! Mom needs you."

Nico was already moving, and Lucia followed him inside, dropping her bag by the door.

The house was in chaos. Oakley stood at the bottom of the stairs, still wearing her school uniform, her face scrunched with worry. The kitchen showed evidence of an attempted meal, with abandoned ingredients on the counter, and a pot boiling over on the stove.

Step one: prevent imminent danger.

"I've got the stove," Lucia shouted, moving toward the kitchen.

Nico nodded and took the stairs two at a time.

In the kitchen, she turned off the burner, wiped up the spill, then looked at her niece. Oakley had grown so much since Christmas. Her face was losing its baby roundness, and her legs were getting longer. She'd be tall like Nico.

"Hey, Oak," Lucia said gently. "Rough day?"

Oakley's bottom lip trembled. "Mom's sick again. She won't eat, and Daddy's worried even though he pretends he's not. I asked if the baby was going to make Mom die, like my first mom died, and Daddy got weird."

"Oh, honey." She crossed the kitchen toward Oakley and pulled her in for a tight hug. "Your mom isn't going to die. It's just morning sickness, which is totally normal when you're pregnant. Uncomfortable, but normal."

"Are you sure?"

"I'm sure. Maddie is healthy and strong. Your little brother or sister is just fine in there."

Oakley held tight for another moment before she pulled back.

"I'm glad you're here, Aunt Lucia. Everything's better when you're here."

The words hit harder than they should have. This little girl, who barely knew Lucia before Maddie came into their lives, now looked at her like she belonged here. Like she was family. The problem was that Lucia was starting to believe it too.

And I have absolutely no idea what to do about it.

PREVIEW: THE
HOLLOW PACK

After her aunt's death, Lena Barkstone retreats to the quiet town of Hollow Creek, hoping grief will fade among towering pines and slow, sleepy nights. Instead, she finds herself watched by wolves, warned away from the woods after dark, and haunted by a moon-shaped necklace her aunt left behind.

Hollow Creek is hiding something, and so was her aunt.

Drawn into a world of shifting loyalties and ancient magic, Lena discovers she stands at the center of a growing war between the mortal world and the Otherwood. Three men are bound to her fate: Atlas, the brooding alpha sworn to protect his pack at any cost; Rowan, the tattooed bartender whose steady presence grounds her when magic spirals out of control; and Silas, quiet, watchful, and dangerously attuned to secrets no one else can hear.

As the boundary between worlds begins to fracture, Lena learns her power isn't something she can walk away from, and neither is the bond forming between her and the wolves who guard her. The Otherwood is waiting. Watching. And it wants her.

The men sworn to protect her may be her greatest strength or the very thing the darkness uses to claim her.

About the Author

Kelsey Karson is a lifelong romantic who believes love always finds a way, no matter the odds. Married and living with her two dogs, she writes emotionally driven romances that explore forbidden attraction, societal boundaries, and the courage it takes to choose love when the world says you shouldn't. Whether her characters are defying expectations or fighting impossible circumstances, Kelsey's stories celebrate passion, resilience, and the belief that no rule is stronger than the heart. Through her work, she invites readers to believe in love without limits and to let no one else define how or whom you love.

www.KelseyKarson.com

ALSO BY KELSEY KARSON

Hollow Series

Hollow Inheritance

Hollow Anchor

Hollow Threshold

Hollow Pact

Timber Ridge

Christmas with a Bear Shifter

Carved in Timber Ridge

Return to Timber Ridge (October 2026)

Her Mountain Christmas (November 2026)

Stand Alone

Temptation

www.ingramcontent.com/pod-product-compliance
Lightning Source LLC
Chambersburg PA
CBHW032008240626
47153CB00003B/1168